The Lipstick Murders

By

Ricky Corum

ISBN-13: 978-1501060779
ISBN-10: 1501060775

Revision (2) September 2019

ii

DEDICATION

This book is dedicated to my best friend for forty-five years Richard "Dickie" Ryan who lost his battle with cancer.

CONTENTS

The characters and events in this book are fictitious. Any similarity to real persons, living or dead, is coincidental and not intended by the author.

ACKNOWLEDGMENTS

Special thanks to my wife Chrissy, without you, life would not exist.

PROLOGUE

THE YOUNG KILLER STOOD at the kitchen counter listening to the five o'clock news. He hoped that today would be special, it was his Mother's 68th birthday. He had picked-up some ice cream for later, but for now, he was going through his daily routine of carrying food to her bedside. She had been fighting a losing battle with cancer for the past year and lately her pain had become unbearable.

He placed a bowl of chicken noodle soup on her tray and fixed himself a ham sandwich. He wanted to enjoy dinner with her and reflect on better times. Sitting on the edge of the bed he began talking to her, but didn't expect her to answer, she rarely speaks anymore. Sometimes, when he stares into her eyes, he believes he can see death, which is a sure sign that she's given-up.

He offered her a spoon of soup, but she turned her head away, which infuriates him. He tried to insert a straw in her mouth for a protein drink and she turned her head again.

Although he loved his Mother at times he wondered, *if she would be better off dead, at least then her suffering would be over.* Suddenly, a sick feeling came over him and his pulse wouldn't stop hammering. His dark side was bursting through and he could feel the rage welling-up inside.

Sitting his cherry soda down, his heart was pounding so hard that he could feel the thumping in his head. Tonight, was the night he thought as he clutched a pillow placing it over her face? He squeezed the pillow tight thinking, *am I really going to do this?* Yes, I am!

At first, she struggled, but didn't put up too much of a fight. He was sure that she had stopped breathing and begins to pull the pillow away when suddenly; she gave one last gasp, which startled him. He nearly fell off the edge of the bed, but he was getting closer to his first moment of glory, his first kill.

Finally, he pulled the pillow from her face and threw it to the side. Could this be a dream? No, he knew it wasn't a dream, it was the real deal, and he had done it.

For several minutes he studied the peaceful look on her face and thought, *finally she's looks content.*

Her nightgown had become tousled and slipped down exposing her chest. Leaning over, he kissed her on the upper part of her left breast and whispered, "Goodbye Mom, I love you with all my heart and I couldn't let you go on suffering any longer."

Glancing down, he noticed that the cherry soda had left a set of red lip marks on her chest where he had kissed her. Getting up from the side of the bed, he ambled to the kitchen for a damp cloth. Returning to her bedside, he began wiping away the marks and then called the police.

The paramedics arrived and he explained to them that when he went to her bedside to feed her, she wasn't breathing. She had terminal cancer and a do-not-resuscitate order.

After confirming that she was dead the paramedics contacted the coroner's office to pick up the body. The young killer watched as they loaded his mother onto the gurney thinking, *I'll have her cremated, that way no one will ever know I killed her.*

There was no trace of tears in his eyes or any track marks on his reddening face. His eyes were narrowed, ridged and hard and in that moment, he was far away. That was the beginning.

CHAPTER 1

September 25, 1979

SUE MARTIN HAS beautiful long blond hair with midnight blue eyes and the true butt of a cheerleader. She's five six with nice perky little breasts that he often catches himself staring at. She wears just the right amount of make-up and he especially likes the bright red lipstick.

Sean's Brooks is six feet tall and wire thin. No one feature made him handsome, although his hazel eyes came close. He never misses a pep rally prior to the Friday night football game and always sits in the bleachers where Sue's cheering. Fixated on her, he begins to smile thinking back to the day they had first met. They were both in the eleventh grade and he had been sitting in the corner all alone at a high school dance when she approached him, "Hi, I'm Sue, can I sit with you?"

"Of course, I'm Sean, nice to meet you," he replied.

"Why are you sitting here all alone?" she asked.

"I don't have any friends, what's your story?" he responded.

"Well, I just transferred to Frederick High and I haven't made any friends yet," she answered.

"Well you have your first," he said reaching out his hand.

"Where were you going to school before you transferred Sue?"

"I've bounced around to a few different schools because I've been in several foster homes."

"How'd you end up in a foster home?" he asked with a puzzled look on his face.

"My parents were killed in a car accident when I was only ten years old and I've been in the system ever since. I don't get along with my foster parents in fact I hate them, they're very strict and verbally abusive. I can't wait until I turn eighteen, so I can get my own place. What about you?" she replied.

"I never really knew my Father, he left my Mother when I was two years old and my Mother died about a year ago." he explained. They talked for hours and he couldn't believe how he had opened-up to her, it was something he had never done before with anyone else. He wanted to ask her to dance but was too bashful.

She kept leaning in to talk over the loud music and he was tempted to kiss her but was afraid of how she might react. The dance was nearly over when she leaned in and she said, "I've got to get going, are you going to kiss me or not."

Their lips met, and it really wasn't much of a kiss, more like a touch of the lips, but to him it was special. Although he was sixteen, it was the first time he had ever been kissed, other than his second cousin when he was ten, but that probably doesn't count. They said their goodbyes and planned to meet the next day for lunch.

Sean was restless, tossing and turning, dreaming of those bright blue eyes, the silky skin and other unexplored places. He woke-up twice in the middle of the night, his heart pounding, *okay-I like her, there, I've admitted it to myself.* He scolded himself and punched the pillow and tried to go back to sleep.

Throughout the eleventh grade they occasionally meet for lunch and became close friends, but Sean wanted more. He asked her to go on a date several times and was embarrassed and upset when she repeatedly turned him down. Today was no different when he had asked her to go to a movie, she said no. *She always seems to have a goddam excuse, I don't care, and I'm never going to stop asking.*

Over the summer between the eleventh and twelfth grade Sean got a job and had only seen Sue a few times. Their first day back to school, he noticed that she had grown in all the right places. She was even more beautiful than he had remembered at the end of the school year. He made his way over to where she was standing with a group of people and asked, "Hey Sue, can I talk to you for second."

"Sure," she replied.

"Can we get together for lunch today and catch up?" he asked.

"No Sean, I already have plans and I've got to get going, I'm going to be late for class." she responded.

"Ok, I guess I'll talk to you later."

He turned to walk away and begin thinking, *something's off; she hardly even talked to me, around those other people. Maybe they're her new friends and she doesn't need me anymore?*

4

CHAPTER 2

March 15, 1982

SEAN WAS WORKING the night shift six to eleven that he hated, but he was finally getting used to it. He thought his job was boring, but he often reminded himself, *at least I get to meet lot of chicks.*

It was quarter to six when he climbed into his white 1972 Chevy van and headed west on Route Forty towards work. He had been working about a half hour making his rounds, when he glanced into a department store and saw her, Sue Martin, the girl of his dreams. He wanted to go up and start talking to her, but he was hesitant. She had shot him down so many times in the past year. *The problem is, she just doesn't know how much I care for her and that we're meant to be together.*

Eventually, he forced himself to walk over and began talking to her. "Hey Sue, how are?" he asked.

"I'm great Sean, how have you been?

"I'm good, what have you been up to since you graduated?"

"I'm going to dental school in York, Pennsylvania, I'm studying to be a dentist," she responded.

Suddenly, he had the strangest feeling that Sue seemed nervous. She kept looking around as if she didn't want anyone to see her talking to him. She was nice enough, but just like in their senior year, she seemed to want to get away from him as fast as possible.

Unexpectedly, a guy approach Sue and said, "Are you ready to go, babe."

Sean had seen the guy before but didn't really know him. Sue turned sideways and said, "Sean, I'd like you to meet my fiancé, Tim Main. We've been dating for a while and recently he proposed to me and I've accepted."

"When's the wedding?" Sean asked, trying to hold back the tears.

"We've planned a long-term engagement, so I can finish dental school," Sue explained.

Sean reached out and shook Tim's hand congratulating him and said, "Well, I'd better be getting back to work."

Sean walked away, and the tears begin to trickle down his cheeks. She was the only person that he had ever loved besides his mother, *why couldn't she love him?*

Tonight, seemed to be going especially slow and boring and he couldn't wait for eleven o'clock to get here. When he finally clocked out, he thought, *it wouldn't hurt to ride by Sue's house; she's probably in bed anyway.* Turning onto Culler Avenue he slowed down looking to the left side of the street and to his amazement, there was a light on the second floor. Carefully, he pressed down on the gas pedal to speed passed her house hoping that she hadn't notice him driving by.

Turning off Culler Avenue he headed west towards home. Outside of his trailer sitting in the driveway, he was cursing himself and thinking how stupid that was. Suppose she'd noticed him driving by, she would have thought he was stalking her and might have called the police.

Climbing out of the van, he went inside the trailer and grabbed a beer from the refrigerator. Going towards the rear of the trailer he glanced up at the wall in front of the bed where he had installed a large wooden cabinet. It was a bulletin board with doors about four-foot-high and four-foot wide. Unlocking it, he swung both doors open wide. Inside the cabinet were pictures of his Mother and Sue Martin plastered all over the bulletin board attached with stickpins.

Propping up some pillows, he kicked off his shoes and slid on the edge of the bed staring up at the pictures. He had taken lots of pictures of Sue with a long-distance camera lens, none of which she knew about.

He began to drift off into a daydream and wished things could have turned out different. He thought about, *his vision from the first day they had met. He believed that they would develop their relationship into something special and someday get married. But that was never going to happen now she had met someone.* Finally, he reasoned, *the best thing I can do for now is to watch and wait and maybe someday she'll be mine.*

Sean followed them for weeks that turned into months trying to figure out what he could do to break them up without turning her against him. He even considered killing Tim; after all, he had killed before and gotten away with it.

Sue and Tim went for long walks to the lake, sit on the benches and fed the ducks. Sean would watch with envy and resentment that *should be me over there sitting next to Sue, hugging and kissing her.*

Then one day, low and behold, Tim was missing from the picture.

Sean couldn't believe his luck; the one thing that had been standing between them was gone. He wondered if, *they had broken up or if something had happened to Tim.*

Two weeks later Sean accidently ran into Sue at McDonald's of all places. He ordered his meal; turned to step back to wait for his order and nearly ran into her. Without even thinking he said, "Hey Sue, how are you? It's been a long time since I've seen you."

It was a good that he didn't have time to think about what to say, because he would have lost his nerve. They made small talk for a few moments and Sue volunteered that her and Tim had broken up.

"Would you like to go out to dinner with me? My Mother's birthday is coming up on Monday and you can help me celebrate," Sean asked in a pleading voice.

"Look Sean, I'm sorry but we're never going to be more than friends. I think you always read more into our relationship then there was. I just wanted to be your friend that was it. That's why I stop hanging out with you, you were way too possessive, and it freaked me out. We can continue to be friends but I'm not going to go out with you on a date, not now, not ever. I just don't have those kinds of feelings for you. I am sorry! I hope you understand."

Sean glanced around the room at all the people staring and said, "but Sue, I love you, I've always loved you and someday you will love me too."

"Grow up, Sean, you are living in a dream world, you can't make someone fall in love with you, I've got to go."

Sue turned and swiftly walked away not daring to look back. He couldn't believe it she had shot him down again, in front of thirty people in a restaurant.

CHAPTER 3

August 24, 1982

SEAN HAD ORDERED a dozen roses and was scheduled to pick them up at 4:00 p.m. on Monday. His plan was to deliver them to Sue and apologize for their little miss understanding.

He hadn't left his trailer for two days and couldn't stop daydreaming about his big plan. He hoped their celebration would end with them setting on her couch kissing. But the other vision was of Sue slamming the door in his face, *I have no idea how it's going to turn out, but I need to give it one last shot.*

Sean was out of bed before 6:00 a.m. on Monday morning. He cleaned the trailer better than it had ever been cleaned before thinking all the while, *you never know, maybe I can talk Sue into coming to see my trailer.*

He drove to the mall to his favorite clothing store and picked up a new outfit for tonight. Entering the store, he purchased a new pair of tan pants, a pair of brown shoes, a light tan shirt and a red button up sweater.

Leaving the mall, he headed off to the flower shop to pick up the flowers he had ordered. Strolling back to the van, smelling the flowers, he was thinking, *Sue is going to love these I know she will.* Carefully, he laid the flowers on the passenger seat of the van, walked around and climbed into the driver's side.

Driving back home, he carried his new outfit inside the trailer, took a quick shower, and got dressed. Part of his plan for the evening was to treat himself to a nice dinner in honor of his Mother before delivering the flowers.

Exiting the trailer, he climbed into the van and twenty minutes later was parked in front of a restaurant. He seemed to be in a daze, thinking about his Mother and how much he missed her.
Today marked four years since the day he'd killed her, and he often woke up in a cold sweat reliving that day.

Finally, he ascended from the van and sauntered inside the restaurant, approached the hostess and said, "I'd like a table for two." The hostess took his name down and told him there would be at least a forty-five-minute wait. "That's fine, I'm in no hurry," he replied.

Nearly an hour had passed when the hostess finally called his name and led him to a table near the back of the restaurant. A few minutes later the waitress introduced herself, "I'm Cathy and I'll be taking care of you, can I get you a drink."

"Yes, I'd like to order a martini and a beer," he replied.

A few minutes later the waitress returned with the drinks, set them on the table and asked, "will someone be joining you?"

"No, I'm just paying my respects to my Mother by ordering her a drink, we would always go out to dinner on her birthday until she died four years ago."

"I'm sorry for your lost, can I take your order now or do you need more time?"

"I'm ready to order, I'll take two salads, two baked potatoes, two steaks cooked medium well, and some bread," he replied.

A short time later the waitress delivered his food and he began savoring every delicious bite. Later the waitress returned and took his empty plate leaving the untouched plate. She supposed, *if this guy's ordering food for someone who's been dead for four years, he may be a little crazy so I'm not going to do anything to antagonize him.*

After dinner, he had decided to chill for a while and drink a few more beers to build up his courage. It was nine-thirty when he finally left the restaurant and drove through town seemingly catching every light. Turning left onto Culler Avenue he parked down the street from Sue's house.

Climbing out of the van he strolled to the passenger side opened the door and picked up the flowers. Straightened them a little, he turned and meander up the street towards Sue's house. Crossing the street, he approached the sidewalk leading to her front porch. Stepping-up on the porch, he reached out with his hand nervously shaking and rang the doorbell.

Sue had been enjoying a quiet evening watching TV when she heard the doorbell. A little startled, she threw her hand to her chest, stood up and glanced around the curtain on the sidelight of the front door. There was a man standing on her front porch and when she looked more intently, she realized it was Sean Brooks.

What the hell does he want? She wondered, just the sight of him standing on her front porch knocked the breath right out of her.

"Who is it?" she asked, pretending not to know.

"It's me, Sean Brooks, I wanted to apologize for our misunderstanding the other day and I brought you some flowers, please open the door."

Reluctantly, Sue unlocked the door and slightly opened it, but only a few inches. She began to smile, but then thought better of it.

"Sean, this is very nice of you, but you shouldn't have."

"I wanted to see you Sue, I've been in love with you since the eleventh grade and I know that you love me too."

"No", Sue blurted out, I told you, I don't think of you in that way, we're just friends, how many times do I need to tell you that? What the hell do I need to do, to get that through to you? Please leave me alone, I've tried to be nice, are you stupid or what?"

Sue started to close the door when Sean yelled, "what the fuck did you say?" He pushed hard against the door swinging it wide open and quickly stepped inside slamming the door shut. Sue fell backwards hitting her head on the coffee table breaking the glass. Lying on the floor with her head bleeding, she was shocked by what had happened. She began to scream, and Sean leaped to where she had landed on the floor grabbing her around the throat.

"Why couldn't you have just loved me? I would have done anything for you, are you even capable of love? I'm going to put you out of your misery," he said as he tightens both hands around her neck. Sue squirmed and tried to fight back, but there was no getting out of his grip and soon there was no movement left in her body.

Finally, he pulled his hands from her throat, looking down with tears in his eyes, he leaned over and kissed the top of her left breast whispering, "Goodbye Sue, I love you with all my heart and I couldn't let you go on suffering any longer."

Sue's purse had fell off the coffee table on the floor scattering everything. Sean noticed a tube of lipstick lying on the floor, grabbed it and drew a set of lips on the upper part of Sue's left breast. He scrambled to his feet and stood there, staring at Sue Martin, the love of his life. There was no trace of tears in his eyes or any track marks on his reddening face. His eyes were narrowed ridged cold and, in that moment, he was already far away.

CHAPTER 4

SUDDENLY, SEAN HEARD a distant voice in his head, it was his mother's voice, "clean up this mess and get the fuck out of there now!"

Flipping the coffee table up, he carefully wiped it off to make sure he hadn't left any fingerprints. He gathered everything up that had fallen from Sue's purse and placed it on the edge of the couch. Entering the kitchen, he found a broom, and begins sweeping up the broken glass and flowers that had scattered on the floor. "*All done*," he said.

Taking one last look around the room he noticed a set of false teeth on the floor under the coffee table. Kneeling, he picked them up and placed them on the end table near the phone. Turning out the lights, he peeked through the front door sidelight. He knew he had to get out of there but spent the next several minuets going back and forth between the front door sidelight and the side window.

Thoughts were rushing through his head *he would need to get rid of the body where no one would ever find it. Would someone report her missing? She had told him that she hadn't spoken to her foster parents for more than a year and Tim Main was out of the picture. If I can just find a place to hide the body, I might be ok.*

Wiping the sweat from his forehead, he opened the front door and quickly ambled down the street to where he had parked the van. Unlocking the driver's side, he jumped in and placed the trash bag with the broken glass and roses on the passenger seat.

Starting the engine, he drove up to the end of the street and continued over to the next street to turn around. Turning back on Culler Avenue he drove down the street and stopped in front of the sidewalk leading to Sue's house.

He got out of the van, went to the passenger side and opened the sliding door. Hurrying back inside the house, he leaned over and picked up Sue's limp body and put her left arm around his neck. He was carrying her with his right arm around her waist as if she was drunk. Lifting the body inside the van, he quickly jumped in and covered her with a painter's drop cloth. Gently he closed the sliding door trying not to make a sound.

He went around to the driver's side and climbed in the van, started it and drove away.

Looking down at the speedometer he realized that he was driving to slow. He'd was trying to be careful not to speed or break any laws because the last thing he wanted was to get pulled over with a dead body in his van.

Finally, he turned into his driveway and sat there for several moments trying to figure out what to do next. *I know there's no way I can take the body out of the van here and carry it inside my trailer. Besides what would I do with her once I got her inside?*

Glancing back to the rear of the van he said, "Holy Fuck," to himself as he noticed Sue's foot was sticking out from underneath the drop cloth. Climbing in between the seats he quickly covered up her foot, neatly tucking the drop cloth underneath.

He got out of the van, locking the door and went inside the trailer. Sitting on the edge of the bed he was sweating like crazy, trying to figure out what he could do with the body. His mind was racing back and forth when he glanced down at the floor seeing an old rug and thought, *no way too small.* Glancing around the trailer, suddenly he saw it sitting at the foot of the bed. It was a trunk that he had recently purchased to store extra blankets in.

Jumping up, he jerked the lid open and started pulling out the blankets throwing them on the bed. Picking up the trunk, he carried it out the front door to the rear of the van.

He glanced around the trailer park to ensure no one was around. Unlocking the rear doors, he opened them, and slid the trunk into the back of the van next to Sue's body. He then climbed into the driver's seat and backed out of the driveway.

He had been driving for about thirty minutes up through the mountain road at Gambrill State Park when he noticed a small clearing and pulled over to the side of the road.

Climbing between the seats into the back of the van, he opened the trunk, picked up Sue's body and placed her inside the trunk. He started to close the lid when it caught a button on his red sweater pulling it off. The button dropped inside the trunk, but it was too dark to see anything.

Suddenly, Sean saw a light through the passenger window up at the end of the lane where he had pulled over.

He quickly climbed back into the driver's seat and pulled off. He wanted to find a spot to hide the body back in the woods far enough that no one would ever find it.

Finally, he saw a clearing and pulled the van over as far as he could to the side of the road. He jumped out and ran around to the rear doors of the van and pulled both doors open. He tried to pick up the trunk, but it was way too heavy. Jerking it out of the back of the van he let it drop to the ground.

He was trying not to panic as the adrenalin was rushing through his veins. Going to one end of the trunk he grabbed the leather handle and began pulling it with all the strength that he could muster. After dragging it twenty feet he started to think, *what if someone comes along? I've got to get the hell out of here.*

Gathering some branches and limbs, he began to throw them on top of the trunk as fast as he could. Running back to the van, he got in and drove away, eventually winding up back at his trailer.

The next day, he read in the newspaper that a body had been discovered at Gambrill State Park in a trunk, but they hadn't identified the body. For months, he couldn't eat or sleep, he worried that the cops or the FBI would come knocking on his door any day. But eventually, a week had passed, and then a month, and he soon began to realize that he had gotten away with another murder.

CHAPTER 5

August 25, 1982

IT WAS APPROXIMATELY 7:00 a.m. when the Frederick Police Department (FPD) received an emergency phone call stating that a body had been discovered in a trunk at the Frederick Watershed.

Police Officers from FPD were dispatched to assist with securing the crime scene. The dispatcher also contacted the Frederick County Sheriff's Department and the Maryland State Police (MSP).

Rookie Police Officer Faye-Lynn Johnson is a strong, beautiful black female who has been a member of the FPD for approximately twelve weeks, nine of which were spent at FPD's new Training Academy.

When she received the call about a homicide, she was already up and dressed. She was wearing her usually tight patrolman's uniform, with the two top buttons undone, showing just enough cleavage to be incredibly sexy. She had short black hair and was wearing bright red lipstick.

Officer Johnson was once married and became pregnant a year later, which suddenly changed her whole world. She had been going to college, studying to be a lawyer and decided to drop out to have the baby. In her sixth month she had a miscarriage and lost the baby. Unfortunately, her marriage went downhill from there and after trying unsuccessfully to mend things, they finally decided to file for a divorce. The divorce became final fifteen weeks ago and a week later she enrolled in FPD's Training Academy.

I've been on the job for two weeks and I've just been dispatched to my first crime scene and it's a murder. To say that I'm a little excited is probably the understatement of the year. Exiting the house, I jumped into my squad car and took off. I could feel the adrenaline rushing through my body and it was awesome.

I was the first to arrive and spoke briefly with the couple that had discovered the body. I then asked them to sit in the back seat of my squad car and wait for the detectives to arrive.

Clutching a pair of rubber gloves from my back pocket, I pulled them on as I walked towards the trunk. My heart was pounding harder and harder with each step closer to the trunk.

I glanced around the outside of the trunk for evidence but didn't see anything. Grabbing the lid with both hands I opened it and couldn't believe my eyes, it was the first dead body I had ever seen. I stood staring at the beautiful young blonde and began to tear up wondering, *why anyone would want to kill her.* I noticed that a set of lips had been drawn on the upper part of her left breast with lipstick.

I heard another vehicle approaching and quickly closed the lid. Removing my rubber gloves, I stuffed them inside my back pocket. I could see a Maryland State Police vehicle rapidly approaching. The vehicle pulled behind my squad car and stopped.

A large man who was bald and wearing black framed glasses climbed out of the vehicle, "Hi, I'm detective Joe Donavan with the MSP, I've been assigned as lead detective on this case."

"I'm officer Faye-Lynn Johnson form FPD, I was dispatched to help secure the scene and I was the first to arrive," I explained.

"Nice to meet you officer Johnson, did you start a Murder Log Book yet?"

"No Sir, all I have are a few notes that I've written down in my notebook."

Detective Donavan walked towards his car, opened the trunk and pulled out a three-ring binder. He handed it to me he said, "Please write down everything in this official murder log book. Start with the time you received the call and go forward until I arrived. When that's complete, I'll sign into the log book and take possession as ranking officer."

"Yes sir, no problem," I replied.

"Who discovered the Body?" Detective Donavan asked.

"Tom and Ellen Ridgeway, that's them over there in the back seat of my car."

"I'll need to ask them a few questions, but then I'd like you to take them to MSP's headquarters, to get a written statement."

"Sure, no problem," I replied.

Ten minutes later I climbed into my squad car and drove the two witnesses to MSP's HQ. As I pulled away from my first crime scene I wondered, *about those lips drawn on the victim's breast, why in the world would someone do that, what could that possibly mean?*

CHAPTER 6

I TURNED INTO MSP parking lot located at the corner of Bachman's Lane and West Patrick Street. I entered the building with Tom and Ellen Ridgeway and explained to the desk sergeant who they were and why we were there. Getting up from his desk, he escorted them down a long hallway into interview room number one.

After closing the door, he turned to me and said, "you don't need to hang around Officer Johnson, I'll keep an eye on the witnesses until detective Donavan gets here."

"Thanks, but if you don't mind, I'd like to stick around and listen to the interview."

"Sure, no problem," he replied and headed back towards his desk.

Forty-five minutes later Detective Donavan finally arrived to begin a more detailed interview with the couple that had discovered the body. I watched through the one-sided mirror as he entered the room. Reaching up to my right I turned on the speaker as he began to talk, "First let me thank you for coming in to HQ to give your statement, your information is extremely important to us."

"No problem," Tom replied.

"What were you guys doing out there walking down that dirt road?" Detective Donavan asked.

"We live about two miles down the road and we were out hunting mushrooms," Tom replied.

"Tell me more about how you discovered the trunk," Detective Donavan instructed.

"We were just walking down the side of the road when we noticed the trunk about twenty feet from the edge. We went over to get a closer look and it was kind of rugged looking with a flat top. It had two leather straps around the outside with decorative metal corners and was tuck in between two small trees. It appeared that someone had started to cover it with branches, but something must have scared them off before they could finish," Ellen stated.

"What did you guys do next?" Detective Donavan asked.

"I tried to open the trunk, but it was locked so I began hitting it with a small rock and finally it popped open.

We raised the lid and when we saw that young girl, Ellen lost it and began screaming. I quickly dropped the lid and spent the next several minutes trying to calm her down. Then, I asked her to go to the neighbor and call the police while I stayed with the trunk," Tom explained.

"Do you remember anything else?" the Detective asked.

"The inside of the trunk was lined with a fabric that had a decorative paisley type design and I saw a black button lying next to her leg, that seemed out of place," Ellen responded.

"Why do you think it was out of place?" the Detective asked.

"Well, because she was wearing jeans and a tank top, nothing with buttons," Ellen replied.

"There's one other thing Detective, when I opened the trunk, there was a reflection from the sun on the back of the girl's tank top. It appeared to be broken pieces of glass and the sun made a reflection, causing it to glitter like diamonds," Tom detailed.

"Did you guys know the victim, was she from around the area?" Detective Donavan asked.

"No, we didn't know her, we've never seen her before today," Ellen replied.

"Did you notice any suspicious activities last night?" Detective Donavan asked.

"No, I'm afraid we were in bed by nine and slept through the night," Tom replied.

Detective Donavan went on for another thirty minutes with countless more questions. He then asked them to please wait while he typed up their statement, so they could sign it. When he came out of the interview room, he nearly ran into me standing near the one-sided mirror. "Oh, you're still here officer, great, could you hang around a little while longer and give the Ridgeway's a ride home?"

"Sure, no problem," I replied.

I drove the ridgeways home and decided to go back to the murder scene again. I parked my car, climbed out and walked over to the site where the trunk had been sitting. The trunk and the body were long gone by now, but I wanted to take one last look. I noticed some tire tracks on the side of the road and wondered if the MSP's crime lab had taken moldings of them?

Finally, I convinced myself there was nothing else to see and headed back to my car. Driving down the dirt road towards Frederick I began day-dreaming, *whishing I was a detective working this case, but I've only been on the force for twelve weeks, so a detective's shield will have to wait, at least for now.*

Two weeks later I called Detective Donavan to inquire about the status of the case. "Hello Detective, sorry to bother you, but I was wondering how the lipstick murder case is going?"

"The Lipstick murder case, that's an interesting name Officer Johnson, you must have opened the trunk at the murder scene?" the detective questioned.

"Yes, I'm sorry, I know I'm not a detective and I probably shouldn't have."

"That's right you shouldn't have tampered with a crime scene and by the way we haven't release that information to the public, so can I count on you to keep it to yourself?"

"Of course," I replied.

"Anyway, we still haven't identified the body, so we have no leads and the case is going nowhere fast," Detective Donavan explained.

"It's really weird that she hasn't turned up on a missing person's report."

"We've been checking that every day, but nothing so far. You seem pretty interested in this case Officer Johnson?"

"I guess I am, after seeing that beautiful young girl dead and stuff inside a trunk, it broke my heart, I just hope you catch the bastard who did it."

"Hopefully, something will turn up soon," Detective Donavan replied.

"I'll let you go for now detective, but I'd like to call you from time to time to keep-up on the case if you don't mind."

"I think that'll be fine."

"I made it a point to call every few weeks to check on the case but after nearly a year the status of the case was officially changed from an active case to a cold case. Sadly, I understood, that this probably meant that this case would never be solved.

CHAPTER 7

August 24, 1986

SEAN BROOKS CONTINUED WORKING as a security guard at the Frederick Shopping Mall and had met someone special. Her name was Stacy Rodgers; she had long blond hair, beautiful blue eyes, and a striking body. He often thought, *she reminds me of Sue Martin, my first true love.* She worked in one of the clothing stores at the mall and they had been friends for nearly two years. He had given her a ride home a few times and had developed a serious crush on her. Lately, he had been trying to work up the nerve to ask her out and would often stop by the store where she worked to talk.

Arriving at work, he stopped to say hello on his first round and had decided to ask her to go out with him for a drink after work tonight. Her store closed at ten, but it was usually eleven by the time she finished counting the day's receipts. It was a special day for him and surly she wouldn't turn him down today, of all days. It was August the 24th 1986, eight years since his mother's death.

Entering the store where she worked, he started out with their usual small talk, finally getting around to it, he asked, "why don't we go out for a drink after work?" Before she had a chance to respond, he continued, "today's the anniversary of my mother's death and I could use some company."

"Sean, I like you as a friend, but I can't go out with you, I have a boyfriend and he's picking me up after work."

"A boyfriend, you never told me you had a fucking boyfriend."

"You never really asked me Sean."

"Ok, I get it," he said, putting up his hand to end the conversation. He then turned and walked away not looking back. As he exited through the front door, he couldn't help but reflect *another blond-haired bitch just broke my fucking heart. What's wrong with me why can't I meet someone who will love me?"*

He went back to work making his rounds and each time he passed Stacy's store he was getting more and more upset, thinking, *how could that fucking bitch lead me on all this time?* Stacy felt terrible about what happened, but also thought, *maybe now that he knows I have a boyfriend he'll back off.*

19

She had been meaning to tell him for some time, but just hadn't worked up the nerve. She knew Sean had a crush on her, but she had no idea how serious it was.

It was fifteen till eleven when she looked up and saw Sean entering the front door. "I was about to lock up for the night, in fact, I thought I had already locked that door Sean."

"Stacy, I need to talk to you, I can't fucking believe after two years of being friends that you don't have any feelings for me."

Her eyes traveled over him, terror ridden, fixing on his face, "get the hell out of here, so I can lock up and go home Sean. My boyfriend's going to be here any minute."

Suddenly, Sean pulled his gun from the holster and pushed Stacy towards the back of the store. "I told you, we need to fucking talk, now."

Her heart began pounding faster and her knees were shaking, this was a side of Sean that she hadn't seen before. When they entered the storage room, he holstered the gun and said, "Stacy, I love you and I know you love me too."

"Sean, I just don't feel that way about you, I'm sorry."

His ears were ringing, and his head began to pound, that sick feeling in his stomach had returned after four years. It was the same thing Sue Martin had told him all over again and he was crushed.

Her eyes darted back and forth, scanning the room looking for a way out. She made a sudden dash for the stock room door and he grabbed her wrist swinging her backwards slamming her into the wall. "Please," she whimpered, her eyes frozen. "Please don't hurt me."

"The truth is, Stacy, I'm going to save you," he said as he smiled into her quivering face. Before he could even comprehend what, he was doing, he reached out and grabbed her around the neck. Her slender body jolted up with a sudden cry and her eyes flickered like a weak electric bulb. She tried desperately to pull his hands away from her neck, but her strength was no match for his. Within minutes he had choked the life out of her and dropped her limped body to the floor.

Looking down, she was beautiful, with delicate features and so young. He remembered back to when they had first met, how he had been so taken with her.

Kneeling beside her on one knee, he leaned over and whispered, "Goodbye Stacy, I love you with all my heart and I couldn't let you go on suffering any longer."

Kissing her on the upper part of her left breast, he stood up and approached the desk. Opening a drawer, he removed Stacy's purse that he had seen her place there many times before. Rummaging through it, he found a tube of red lipstick and drew a set of lips on the upper part of her left breast.

Tears began to well up in his eyes and suddenly he thought he heard his mother's voice, "clean up this mess and get the fuck out of there, now." His mind began racing, *I'll need to get rid of the body, maybe I can take it up to Gambrill park and dump it like I did Sue's. After all, it's been four years since I killed her, and those idiots never even identified her body.*

Suddenly, there was a noise at the front of the store, *why in the fuck didn't I lock that door when I came in?* He felt trapped and began to panic looking around the room for an escape route. He lunged forward and pushed open the fire door and quickly realized he was in the deserted parking lot at the rear of the shopping mall.

He walked behind the mall eventually making his way back to the front side of the stores at the other end. When he reached Stacy's store, he didn't see anyone milling around outside and was relieved. She must have lied to him about her boyfriend picking her up, because her car was in the parking lot.

He stared through the front windows for several minutes trying to see if there was anyone inside the store. Pulling his gun from his holster, he entered the store and began clearing it section by section, like he had seen in the movies. He wanted to be certain that no one had wandered into the store and discovered the body.

Reaching the storage room, he confirmed that no one else was in the store and picked up the phone to call the police. "Hello, I am Sean Brooks the security guard at the Frederick Shopping Mall and I've discovered a body."

Sean knew he would be considered a suspect, but there was just no other way to handle the situation. If he wouldn't have called the police, that would have raised more suspicion towards him. When they arrived, he explained that he'd noticed that the front door was unlocked. He went inside to check it out and discovered Stacy's Rodgers body in the rear storage room.

CHAPTER 8

August 25, 1986

DECTIVE JOE DOVANAN'S phone began to ring as he glanced over at his alarm clock. 12:01 a.m., *who in the hell is calling me at this hour? I'm not scheduled to go on duty until tomorrow morning at 8:00 a.m."* Grabbing up the receiver he said, "Donavan, what's up."

"Hey Joe, this is the desk Sergeant, I'm sorry to bother you at this time of night, but there's been a murder at the Frederick Shopping Mall and Major Jenkins wants you to get over there right away."

"I'm on days, and besides that's inside the city limits you need to call Detective George Stone over at FPD."

"George is already there but the Major wants you to work the case with him, you'll understand once you get there."

"Ok, no problem, be there in twenty minutes." Detective Donovan replied as he climbed out of bed.

Quickly getting dress, he treads toward the bedroom door when his wife asked, what's going on Joe?"

"There's been a homicide over at the Frederick Shopping Mall, go back to sleep, I'll call you later," Joe whispered, kissing her on the cheek.

He left his apartment on 9th street heading for the murder scene wondering why *he was called in on an FPD case. It did happen from time to time, but not very often.*

Pulling up in front of the store where the murder had taken place there were already several black and whites with lights flashing. He scrambled out of his vehicle and badge his way through the front door. A uniformed officer pointed him towards the rear of the store where several people were standing around talking.

"Hey George, what we got?"

"It looks like a murder by strangulation," he replied.

"Who discovered the Body?" Joe asked.

"The Security Guard, that's him standing over there with the uniformed officers."

"What-you-say, we take him to FPD for questioning."

"Sure, no problem."

"Why'd you call MSP in on this George?

"There something you need to see Joe," George said stepping inside the storage room.

Joe followed and saw the body lying on the floor covered with a white sheet. Crouching down, George pulled back the sheet revealing the victim. "I wanted you to see this before the coroner removes the body."

"Holy shit," Joe blurted out.

What he saw brought back all the memories of the one case that had gotten away from him. The case that after countless hours of work and investigation he couldn't solve and four years later it still haunted him. Joe seemed to be in daze thinking, *what's going on here, is this same killer striking out again? Where in the hell has, he been for four years? Or maybe we just have a copycat?*

"You ok Joe?" George asked.

"I'm fine," he replied, quickly snapping back to reality.

"Is it ok for the coroner to take the body? George asked.

"Not yet, I saw Officer Faye-Lynn Johnson out front securing the scene, please asked her to come back here, I need her to see the body," Joe explained.

"Why would want her to see the body, she's not a detective?" George asked.

"She saw the young girl four years ago and may remember something that I've overlooked," Joe replied.

A few minutes later George entered the storage room with officer Faye-Lynn Johnson.

"Hello officer Johnson, it's been a while," Joe said.

"Yes, it has, Detective Donavan, it's good to see you, but I wish it was under better circumstances," I replied glancing down at the body. "Is there something you need me to do for you Detective?"

"Yes, if you don't mind, I need you to look at the body. Then I'd like for you to take some notes and provide them to me," Detective Donavan explained.

"Sure, no problem," I said, although I was a little confused. Opening my notebook, I squatted down to get a closer look as Detective Donavan drew back the sheet. I saw the red lips drawn on the victim's left breast and everything came into focus. The Lipstick Murderer had struck again.

CHAPTER 9

IT WAS OBVIOUS to Sean Brooks that the police suspected him for Stacy Rodgers murder when they began playing good cop, bad cop during the questioning. Finally, at 4:00 a.m., the good cop, Detective George Stone told him he could leave and thanked him for calling the police when he discovered the young girl's body.

He stood up from the table and suddenly the bad cop, Detective Joe Donavan grabbed his arm, "I believe you had something to do with this girl's death and I'm going to nail your ass to the wall, if it's the last thing I ever do."

Pulling away from the detective grasped, Sean hurried off towards the front door. The two Detectives followed him to the glass doors and watched as he walked across the street and climbed into Officer Johnson patrol car. They had asked her to give him a ride back to the Shopping Mall where his vehicle was parked.

"Well, what you think Joe? Detective Stone asked.

"His story doesn't add up, my gut tells me, he could be our killer, we just need to figure out how to prove it."

"Aren't you jumping the gun?"

"Like I said it's a gut feeling, I think we need to keep a close eye on him, he'll make a mistake sooner or later, they all do."

For the next several months Sean anticipated that one-day the cops would kick-in his front door and arrest him for murder. It seemed like every time he looked over his shoulder, he noticed one of the Detectives following him. They didn't even try to conceal themselves or to pretend to be undercover. He assumed that this was their way of intimidating him and it was working. Lately he had been so upset that he even thought about, confessing and getting it all over with. *I need get the hell out of Frederick if I stayed here this harassment is going to break me.*

Sean hoped that eventually they'd get tired of following him and go away, but after months of harassment he realized that the only way to make it stop was for him to disappear. He had a cousin, Brandon Smith who lived in North Dakota and decided to give him a call. After several rings someone finally pick-up the phone and said, "hello."

"Is this Brandon?"

"Speaking, who's this?"

"It's me, your cousin, Sean.

"Hey man, how are you? I haven't heard from you in ages," Brandon replied.

"I'm ok, but the reason I'm calling is that I've been thinking about moving to North Dakota. A young girl was killed at the shopping mall where I work, and the police think that I had something to do with it. Of course, I didn't, but I can barely stand the harassment anymore and I just need to get the fuck out of Maryland. If I decide to come to North Dakota, can put me up for a few weeks until I find a Job?"

"Sure, come on out, I've got plenty of room," Brandan replied.

"Ok, thanks, I'm not sure when I'll be leaving, but I'll let you know." Sean said and hung up the phone letting out a sigh of relief.

Sean got off work on Thursday night at ten o'clock and when he got home, he noticed a detective from FPD sitting up the street watching his trailer. Climbing out of the van, he looked towards the detective and stuck up his middle finger. As he entered the trailer, he thought, *that's it, that's the last fucking straw.* He went straight to the phone and called Brandon telling him, *"I'll see you in few days. I need to take care of a couple of things and then I'm getting the hell out of Maryland."*

The following day Sean went to work and told his boss that he was quitting his job. He placed a called to his Aunt Jennifer, "Hello."

"Hi, Aunt Jenn, I wanted to let you know that I'm leaving town for a while and I was wondering if you could go by the trailer occasionally to check on my mail. I'll send you some money to keep up the rent at the trailer park in case I decide to come back."

"How long will you be gone?' She asked.

"I don't know it could be a month, six months, at this point I have no idea. I've got to go Aunt Jenn, but thanks, I'll talk to you in a few weeks."

"Ok, goodbye Sean, take care of yourself."

Sean went to his bank and drew out two thousand seven hundred fifty-one dollars from his checking account and forty-seven dollars from his savings account. Returning to his trailer, he grabbed his duffle bag from the closet and started stuffing clothes in it. He then took a plastic bag in the bathroom and gathered-up his medicine.

Entering the kitchen, he retrieved a green garbage bag and another plastic bag. Approaching the wall near the end of the bed he opened the large cabinet doors where his pictures were displayed of his Mother, Sue Martin and Stacy Rodgers. He began removing the pictures one by one and putting them inside the plastic bag.

After removing all the pictures, he bent down on one knee and pulled out a storage container from underneath the bed. Opening the container lid, he pulled out several journals that he often wrote in. He began writing in the first journal in 1978 the day he killed his mother and had been writing in them ever since. These journals described in explicit detail how he had killed his mother, Sue Martin, and Stacy Rodgers.

He began pulling the journals from the storage container and was thinking, *if anyone ever discovered these that would be the end for me.* These were his two most prized possessions, but he had decided it was time to get rid of them. He dropped the journals inside the green trash bag with the pictures.

Looking out the window he didn't see the Detective anywhere in site. Exiting the trailer, he unlocked the Van and threw in his duffle bag. Going back inside the trailer he grabbed the green garbage bag with the pictures and journals. He locked the trailer door and threw the green garbage bag inside the trashcan in front of the trailer.

Climbing in the van he started it, put it in reverse and begins to back out of the driveway when suddenly, he slammed on the brakes. Jumping out of the van, he hurried to the trashcan and grabbed the green trash bag. Going to the side of the van, he opened the sliding door and threw the bag inside thinking, *I supposed I'm not quite ready to get-rid my two most prize possessions just yet.*

CHAPTER 10

THREE DAYS LATER, Sean cruised to a stop in front of his cousin's house. The house was an attractive two story with a red front door and a white picket fence. The wooden porch stretched all the way across the front of the house and had two rocking chairs sitting on it. The sun-lit sky was sending rays that glint brightly across the clear water of the pond next the house and Sean thought, *finally, I might have found the serenity that I've been looking for.*

Grabbing his duffle bag from the Van, he met Brandon who was standing on the front porch waiting to greet him.

"Hey Sean, great to see you," he said as they shook hands.

"Good to be here, this is the most relaxed I've felt for the last three months," Sean replied.

"That's cool man, I'm glad you're here, I can really use the company, it gets pretty lonely out here sometimes."

"I need to find a job, I've got a little bit of money but it's not going to last." Sean explained.

"You can stay with me as long as you want, don't worry about looking for another place we can share the expenses here. Also, I have a good lead on a job for you at the shopping center about five miles down the road."

"Thanks Brandon, I really appreciate it."

"No problem, come-on let me show you your room."

Sean got the job at the shopping center and after a week or two was settling in to a daily routine. Brandon wasn't married or dating anyone, so it was just the two of them in the three-bedroom house and the nearest neighbor was several miles away. Brandon had been working the three to eleven shifts at a clothing factor and Sean was working days as a Security Guard. They hadn't seen much of each other lately and Sean was very lonely longing for someone to talk to.

Time seemed to drag at a snail pace in North Dakota, but Sean realized today he had been there for three months already. Brandon was working, and Sean was sitting on the front porch drinking a beer and listing to the radio. He was flipping the dial back and forth when he came across a Nationwide Confession Hotline. He listened carefully as people called the hot line and anonymously confessed their deepest, darkest sins.

The next five days Sean listen to the hot-line every night and the more he listened to other people's confessions the more he felt the need to confess.

Friday night Sean took a shower, got dress and jumped in his Van. Ten minutes later he was sitting in front of a grocery store staring at the pay phone outside the store. He was debating with himself, "should I do this? I need to tell someone it's eating me up inside," he whispered.

Climbing out of the Van, he approached the phone and his hands were shaking as he dropped the coins into the slots. He dialed the number as an old woman walked by dragging a kid. Turning his back towards them, he slowly began to speak.

"Hello is this the Confession Hot-line?"

"Yes, it is, please tell us your deepest, darkest confession?" the DJ replied.

"My name is John Smith and I'm calling from the mid-west, I know this is going to sound surprising, but I killed someone six months ago. She worked alone in a ladies clothing store and I would often visit with her to talked. The night I killed her we got into a big argument in the storage room and I strangled her. This happened in Frederick Maryland, but I left the State because the police were closing in on me."

The DJ was to shock to speak so he let Sean ramble on not wanting to interrupt. Suddenly, the phone went silent and the DJ ran into the producer's booth and asked, "please tell me you got all that."

"Yes, we got it," the producer responded with a grin giving the DJ a thumb's up.

"We need to get in touch with the police in Frederick Maryland as soon as possible." The DJ blurted out.

Sean hurried back to his Van feeling a tremendous sense of relief. By the time he drove home the hot-line show was over and he was beginning to second-guess what he'd done, *suppose they trace the call? Did I mention Stacy's name? What the fuck was I thinking?*

CHAPTER 11

SEAN BROOKS, THE PRIMARY SUSPECT for the murder of Stacy Rodgers had dropped off the grid and the detectives had no idea where he'd disappeared too. Detective Stone occasionally would drive by Sean's old trailer hopeful that someday he would return.

Turning into the trailer park, he noticed a strange car he'd never seen before parked in Sean's driveway. He pulled directly behind the car blocking it in and quickly climbed out of his police cruiser. Approaching the trailer, he reached out and knocked on the front door. After a few minutes, a very frail old lady with gray hair wrapped in a bun opened the door and said, "can I help you sir.

"Hello mam, I'm Detective George Stone with the Frederick Police Department and I'm looking for Sean Brooks, is he here"

"No, he's not here, I'm his Aunt, he called me a few months ago and asked me to come by and clean his trailer every few weeks."

"Do you know where he is?

"No, I have no idea, why are you looking for him anyway?

"Routine questioning in a case I'm working.

"Well, I have no idea where he is, or when he'll be back.

"Here's my card please give me a call if you hear anything from him, it's very important that I talk with him," Detective Stone said.

Detective Donavan felt certain that Sean Brooks was the killer, but Detective Stone still wasn't convinced. Sean had discovered the body and was the only person at the scene when the FPD arrived on the night of the murder. That automatically made him a prime suspect, but there was no physical evidence connecting him to the murder.

Jimmy Often Stacy's boyfriend was also considered a prime suspect. They had met in high school and dated for over a year. Three weeks prior to the murder Stacy found out that Jimmy had cheated and broken-up with him. Jimmy was calling her practically every day apologizing and trying to get back together.

Stacy had agreed to see him the morning of her death. He arrived at her house around 9:00 a.m. and Stacy led him into the living room where they talked for over an hour. After some back and forth she finally agreed to give him one more chance.

Accepting his high school ring back, she placed it on a gold necklace around her neck.

At first Jimmy's story sounded credible to the detectives, but after interviewing several of Stacy's friends, no one could confirm that the two had gone back together. In fact, some of her friends said he had beaten her up and that was the real reason they had broken up. The detectives tried to do a follow-up interview with Jimmy, but he had also mysteriously disappeared.

The high school ring and necklace were discovered on the floor next to the body and it appeared that the necklace had been ripped from Stacy's neck. The detectives were growing more and more frustrated each passing day because the case had come to a complete standstill. Three months had passed since Stacy's murder and they had no new evidence.

Friday night at approximately 10:15, FPD received a call from the producer of a nationwide radio station. "Hello, is this the Frederick Police Department."

"Yes, how can we help you?"

"This is Pete Horner the Producer of Confession Hot-Line. We had a strange call on our show earlier tonight. Someone confessed to killing a girl in Frederick Maryland who worked in a clothing store. I recorded the conversation and will provide it to you if you can give me the address to send it."

When detectives received the taped, they thought it was going bust the case wide open. They listened to the taped and the caller said, "I killed my girlfriend three months ago on August 24, 1986. I thought about turning myself in to the police, but whatever they do to me won't bring her back. I've decided that I'm going to stay out of Maryland because they have the death penalty in that State. I'm sorry about what I did because I loved her, but she refused to love me back, Bye."

The police reviewed the tape but there was simply no way to prove who the caller was. Time quickly past by and there was never enough evidence to make an arrest. With no new evidence in more than a year the status of the case was officially changed from an active case to a cold case. Six months later Detective Joe Donovan from MSP decided to retire and less than a year later George Stone retired from FPD.

CHAPTER 12

October 15, 1990

SEAN BROOKS STAYED IN North Dakota for nearly three years, and then one day out of the blue he decided it was time to go home. He figured, if the cops hadn't arrested him by now for the murders he'd committed, they never would.

He called his old boss and got his job back as a security guard at the Frederick Shopping mall. Back in Frederick for six months, one afternoon he was driving down East Street when saw a beautiful young girl walking home from school. She had long blond hair and a delicately shaped body with perky little breast. She was wearing blue jeans with a then white blouse and a black jacket. He thought just *for the hell of it, I'm going to ask her if she wants a ride.* He pulled to the curb, put down his window and as she started to walk by, he yelled, "Ha, do you need a lift?"

To his amazement she said, "sure," and hopped into his van without giving it a second thought. He couldn't believe his luck; after all, he was a perfect stranger. He had only driven about twenty blocks from where he had picked her up when she told him to pull over. She pointed and said, "that's my house up there at the end of the street. I don't want my parents to see me getting out of your van, they would get pissed off and probably ground me."

"No problem, I don't want you to get into any trouble. But before you go, we haven't been formerly introduced." Holding out his hand he said, "My Name is Sean Brooks, what's yours?"

She giggled and said, "I'm Tracy Roberts," and shook his hand.

"Can I give you a ride home tomorrow?" he asked.

"Sure, why not, you can pick me up outside the school in the North parking lot at 3:30." She replied.

The next day Sean was outside the school waiting when the 3:30 bell rang and a few minutes later he saw Tracy walking across the parking lot. She waved and smiled. *"Wow,"* he thought, *I haven't had a girl smile at me like that for a very long time.*

He continued picking her up after school practically every day. It was very easy to fit into his schedule because he didn't need to be to work until 6:00 p.m. He was much older than her, but he was happy that the subject never seemed to come up.

When he dropped her off today, he leaned in to kiss her goodbye hoping she wouldn't resist. She didn't, when he leaned towards her, she grabbed the back of his neck and kissed him. It wasn't much more than a touch of the lips, but he loved it. Quickly she jumped out of the Van and said, "see you tomorrow."

As she walked away Sean wondered *could this be real?* "*I think she likes me, she really likes me,*" he mumbled to himself. This went on for several months, but Sean wanted more. He had touched her breast a few times, but she had pushed his hand away. He knew he had to be careful because the last thing he wanted to do was to scare her off.

He had been picking her up every day for nearly five months when one day she told him that she wouldn't need a ride home the next day. She explained that she had gotten into trouble in English class and had to stay after school.

Sean understood, but decided that he was going to show up, wait until she got out of detention and surprise her. He arrived at the school the usual time and parked near the rear of the parking lot. A few minutes later he saw Stacy walkout of the school holding hands with a guy and climb into a brand-new blue corvette. They drove out of the parking lot and Sean followed to see where they were going.

Unexpectedly, they stopped, and Sean quickly pulled to the curb, so they wouldn't see him. It appeared that the guy in the corvette was dropping her off at the same place that he usually dropped her.

Suddenly, she leaned over and kiss him goodbye before getting out of the car. Sean felt a tear trickle down his cheek as his head begin to thump and his chest was beating harder and harder. He pounded down on the steering wheel thinking, *we love each other, why would she do this to me, another blond-haired bitch just broke my fucking heart. What's wrong we me why can't someone love me.*

The next day Sean saw her walking down the street, pulled over and yelled, "Tracy, we need to talk?"

She climbed into the van and Sean drove off towards her house. He pulled to the curb at the usual spot and said, "Stacy, I came to pick you up yesterday and I saw you getting into that blue car, who was that guy anyway, did you even know him?"

"I've known him for several years, we just started dating and he asked me to go steady.

I wanted to tell you, but I didn't know how."

"Tracy, I can't believe you are doing this to me, I love you and I thought you loved me too," he replied.

"I like you Sean, you're my friend, but that's all we are. I just don't think of you in that way and besides you're way too old for me, goodbye," she said swinging the door open and quickly jumping out of the van.

"What the fuck did you just say?" He screeched, reaching out for her. But it was too late she was already out of the van and walking towards her house. He wanted to go after her, but there were to many people walking down the street and he didn't want to make a scene.

As he was driving home, his ears were ringing, and his head began to pound, that sick feeling in his stomach had returned. It was the same thing Stacy Rodgers had told him all over again and he was crushed. He began talking to himself, *"That Fucking Bitch! I thought she was different but she's just like all the others. They lead you on until you fall for them and then break your fucking heart. If I can't have you Tracy, no one will."*

CHAPTER 13

August 24, 1990

SEAN HADN'T SEEN Tracy for several weeks, but he couldn't stop thinking about her. She had graduated, so he couldn't catch her walking home from school anymore. He needed to figure out another way, because he was determined to see her.

Parking his Van down the block from her house one afternoon, he waited three long hours before she finally came out. She was walking down the street in his direction and as she ambled by the passenger window, he shouted, "Hey stranger, how are you?"

"Hi Sean," she responded.

"Where you are heading?"

"I'm going downtown to do a little shopping,"

"Get in and I'll give you a ride," he insisted.

"I don't need a ride, I need the exercise," she replied.

After several minutes of back and forth, she reluctantly climbed into the van. Sean pulled away from the curb and headed up the street passing her house. He turned on to South Street and after passing the Southern Market, turned right on to a dirt road.

Tracy, became agitated and blurted-out, "Sean where in the fuck are you taking me? I told you I wanted to go downtown."

Edging over to the side of the dirt road, he stopped the van and began to explain, "Today's my mother's birthday and we always went out to dinner to celebrate before she died. Will you go out with me tonight?"

"Sean, I told you before, that is never going to happen, we are never going out on a date. How many times do I have to tell you that?"

"Why can't you love me Tracy? Do you think you are too fucking good for me?" he shouted.

Suddenly he grabbed her around the neck, and she began to kicked and squirmed. The crazed look in his eyes terrified her as his grip became tighter. His hands felt like steel as they closed like a vise grip around her neck. She fought back instinctively terrified about what was on the other side. Her nails dug into his skin, but his grip was unyielding. She began to see dark spots across her vision as she became more and more frantic.

She felt herself weaken and asking, *why is he doing this?* Tears were streaming from her eyes and she felt her arms go limp as darkness overcame her sight.

He released his hands from around her neck and she slumped to the floor of the van. The sweat was beading on his forehead and his chest was pounding as he realized what he had done. He glanced up and down the dirt road to make sure no one was around.

Starting the van, he began driving down the road looking for a place to dump the body. He had only driven a short distance and there on the left side of the road was an old couch, some carpet and other garbage, *this is the spot*, he thought.

Stopping the van, he jumped out and quickly un-rolled the carpet on the dirt road. Jerking open the passenger door, he pulled out Tracy's limp body and dragged her to the rear of the van. He laid her down on the edge of the carpet, dropped to his knees, leaned over and kissed her on the upper part of her left breast, "Goodbye Tracy, I love you with all my heart and I couldn't let you go on suffering any longer."

Jumping up, he grabbed Tracy purse from the floorboard and rummaged through it until he found her lipstick. Going back to the body he quickly drew a set of lips on her left breast where he had kissed her goodbye. Dropping her purse on the carpet beside her body, he rolled it up, working it towards the side of the road.

Climbing in the van he drove down the dirt road looking for a place to get back on South Street. Up ahead he saw a turn-off and as he reached it, he noticed two homeless men walking along the side of the road. *Holy Fuck, those guys saw my face! Should I kill them? No, there are two of them and besides I've never killed a man before.* He quickly talked himself out of going back and kept driving.

The next morning, Sean drove to 7-11 and picked up the morning newspaper. There was an article about Tracy's murder, and it stated that two homeless men had discovered the body. He was nervous wreck and couldn't stop thinking, *if the police come around and start harassing me again, I'm not sure I can take it.* All he could think about was the two homeless men, *had they got a good look at him? Maybe they were too drunk to identify him.* He could only hope.

CHAPTER 14

I'D BEEN ON DUTY about an hour working the 3:00 to 11:00 shift when I received the radio call from HQ. The dispatcher explained that two homeless men had discovered a body on a dirt road just off West South Street. My orders were to get over there as soon as possible to secure the scene.

Turning on my siren and lights, I accelerated up West Patrick Street hill heading towards the crime scene. Passing the Southern Market, I took a sharp right and turned on to a dirt road. Off to my left I noticed a hill climb, which included ten or fifteen mounds of dirt space out in a large circle. Local kids often went there to ride their bicycles and dirt bikes, but today it was dormant. Just past the hill climb was a heavily wooded area on the right side of the road where homeless people were known to hangout.

I drove a half-mile further and could see a male uniform officer standing on the side of the road with the two homeless men. I threw my car in park, bolting from it and asked Officer Evan Howell, "Where's the body?"

"It's over there in that pile of garbage rolled up in a piece of old carpet."

I cross the road and the air was ponged with the smell of trash and the sour odor of urine. Fighting my gag reflex, I edged closer to get a better look and saw two feet dangling out from the edge of the carpet. "Shit, I was hoping to get a better look at the body." I cried out to Officer Howell.

"You want to unroll the carpet, Faye-Lynn?"

"No, we need to wait for the detectives and one of us should probably be up at the end of the road to make sure no unauthorize people get back here," I replied.

"OK, I'll go up to the entrance if you want to stay here with the body," Officer Howell replied.

"No problem," I said with a grin.

Officer Howell climbed into his car, turned around and headed up the dirt road towards the entrance. I pulled a notebook from my rear pocket and begin to write some notes.

Approximately fifteen minutes later I heard a vehicle coming down the dirt road and looked up to see an unmarked police cruiser heading towards me.

The vehicle pulled up beside my squad car and two detectives climbed out.

Detective Dominick Thomas is a 6'2, 280-pound black man and very intimidating to look at. He was dressed in a wrinkled-up suit that looked as if he had slept in it for the past three days. He had on a blue necktie that was hanging at least two inches below his collar. He's been with the FPD for more than twenty years and was promoted to a Detective just after Detective George Stone retired.

Detective Thomas partner, Duke Wayne is 5'6, 180 pounds with brown hair and a thinly trimmed mustache. He was well dressed and very well groomed in fact he looked like he could have been a male model. He's only been with FPD for two years and I really don't know him all that well. I once told him that I wanted to be a detective and he offered to help me study for the exam. I figured he was just flirting, but I know he's married so I'm not interested.

Approaching me, Detective Thomas asked, "Hey beautiful, what we got?"

"There's a dead body rolled up in that old carpet over there, but I'm not sure if it's a man or a woman, I didn't want to disturb the crime scene."

"You did the right thing Faye-Lynn, Detective Wayne needs to get some pictures first, then we can un-roll the carpet." Detective Thomas replied.

"Are they the ones who discovered the body? Detective Wayne asked pointing towards the two homeless men.

"Yes, they said they live in those woods back there," I replied.

"Can you keep an eye on them and make sure they don't leave, we need to interview them?" Detective Thomas asked.

"Sure, no problem," I replied.

Detective Wayne began taking pictures from every possible angle and then they carefully un-rolled the carpet revealing the body of a young white female. I was about fifty feet away with the two homeless men and couldn't see much. The coroner arrived and told the detectives that the young girl had only been dead for a few hours. She has no visible track marks and it appears that she died of asphyxiation. I'll need to get her back to the morgue to do a full autopsy. "Here's her purse with her ID, we'll need to notify the next of ken," Detective Thomas detailed to his partner.

I wanted to get a closer look at the body, so I asked the two homeless men to get in the back seat of my car and wait for the detectives to interview them.

Walking over to where the group of men was standing discussing the case I looked down at the young girl's body and was heartbroken. Suddenly, I noticed the red lips drawn on the upper part of her left breast and blurted out, "oh my god."

"What is it Faye-Lynn, what's wrong, do you know her? Detective Thomas asked.

"I'll tell you what wrong, we have a serial killer on our hands. Those lips drawn on her breast are his signature."

I went on to explain to the detectives about the other murders, "Joe Donavan, a detective over at the Maryland State Police was the lead detective on the other cases, but he's retired now. Maybe you should contact MSP to get a copy of those files."

"We will and thanks for the information Faye-Lynn? Please take the two witnesses back to HQ for questioning." Detective Wayne said.

"Ok, no problem I'll see you back there." I said as I turned and walked off towards my squad car.

Leaving another Lipstick murder scene, I couldn't help but wonder, *how many more before we catch the person who's killing these innocent young girls. By my count there's at least three that we know of, could there be more.*

CHAPTER 15

I COULD BARELY STAND the smell of the two half-drunk homeless men who were in the back seat of my car. I couldn't stop gaging and was close to throwing-up my breakfast.

Finally, I turned into HQ's driveway and drove down along the side of the building to the rear parking lot. I climbed out of my car opened the back door and couldn't help but wonder, *if I'll ever get rid of that smell.*

We entered the building, climbed the stairs to the second floor and went to interrogation room number one. I asked the two homeless men to have a seat and wait for the detectives to arrive. I then offered them a soda and a pack of crackers, which they both accepted.

Thirty minutes later the detectives arrived and began their questioning. "Hi, I'm Detective Thomas and this is my partner Detective Wayne. Please tell us what happen earlier today."

One of the homeless men with long hair and a straggly beard began to speak, "we were walking-up the dirt road looking for some cans to sell and came upon a pile of trash with an old sofa and decided to rest. I glanced to the right and saw a carpet rolled-up with two feet dangling out of the end. At first, I thought I was hallucinating, I screamed at my friend to look and said, "I think there's a body in that carpet over there."

"What did you do after that? Detective Wayne asked.

"We un-rolled the carpet to take a closer look, we wanted to make sure it was a real person and not a dummy."

"Wait a minute, you say you un-rolled the carpet and looked at the body?" Detective Thomas asked.

"Yes, and we couldn't believe what we'd found, it was a beautiful young girl. It looked like she had been choked, we could see marks on her neck."

"What did you do next?" Detective Wayne asked.

"We cried, then we decided to roll the carpet back up like we'd found it. I told my friend that I would stay with the body while he went up to the Southern Market and called the police."

"Does anyone else live in the woods out there?" Detective Thomas asked.

"Yes sir, all-together there's seven of us, six men and one woman, we watch out for each other," the homeless man explained.

Detective Thomas approach me standing against the wall and said, "Officer Johnson, go pick up the others and bring them in for questioning."

"No, problem." I replied and called for back up before heading to the wooded area where the other homeless people were staying. We approached their campsite with caution and explained to them what was going on and they all agreed to come back to HQ for questioning.

The questioning of the two homeless men who had discovered the body had gone on for more than an hour and the detectives agreed to rule them out as suspects. They had placed a lot of weight on the fact that they had contacted the police when they found the body. By the time the detectives had finished questioning them Officer Howell and I had returned with the other homeless people.

The detectives interviewed the female and quickly rule her out as a suspect. They then interviewed three other men ruling them out because they had all been together and their stories were consistent.

The last person the detectives interviewed was a mentally ill black man by the name of Ronald Evans. He was 6 foot 2 inches tall and weighs about 220 Lbs. He had recently been released from prison after serving three years of a ten-year sentence.

Ronald couldn't account for his where a bouts at the time of the murder and after his interview, he quickly became a suspect. He had a lengthy rap sheet, which included sex offenses against women. He had been diagnosed several times with severe mental illnesses, including a diagnosis of pedophilia and paranoid schizophrenia.

The Detectives set up surveillance right away and followed him for more than a month without turning up any new evidence. The Chief of Police decided the surveillance was too expensive and discontinued it.

Less than a week later an eleven-year-old girl was sexually assaulted and killed. The young girl was last seen with Ronald Evans at a small grocery store and the body was discovered two blocks away a few hours later. He immediately became the suspect for the eleven-year-old girl's murder and within hours of the murder he was arrested and confessed. He was later convicted of first-degree murder and sexual assault.

After the extensive background investigation of Ronald Evans was complete, the detectives concluded that he had nothing to do with Tracy Roberts' murder. She had not been sexually assaulted so that didn't fit Ronald Evans MO. I agreed with the detectives that Ronald Evans had not killed Stacy Rodgers, but that also means the Lipstick Murderer is still out there somewhere.

On November 4, 1990, Ronald Evans was beaten to death in prison and died at the age fifty-three. The Chief of Police for FPD blamed himself for the death of the eleven-year-old girl and decided to retire.

CHAPTER 16

December 13, 1990

JESSICA GREEN HAS an hourglass figure with long soft brown hair set in curls, dark brown eyes, that go perfectly with her full lips, petite nose and adoring smile. She's dated a couple of guys over the last year, but nothing steady. At the young age of twenty-two she feels everything is going according to plan. She's currently attending two college courses, training to become a store manager and about to purchase a new home.

After searching for weeks, she realized that all she could afford was a Townhome. She found one that she really liked in a new subdivision and wrote a contract to lock-down the purchase.

Today's the big day and she's thrilled to be going to the settlement on her new home in the Meadows Subdivision. She had asked her parents to accompany her and after signing the last document, she looked up to see tears in her Father's eyes. He said, "I'm very proud of you Jessica," leaned over and kissed her on the cheek.

She thanked both her parents for providing the money for the down payment. She knew that without their help she wouldn't have been able to buy the house. As they were getting up from the table Jessica's father said, "Let me take you to lunch to celebrate."

"I can't Dad, in fact I need to run, my furniture's coming, and I have to be at work by three, it's my night to close the store." She explained.

Her father grimaced at the thought of her closing the store and although he knew she loved her job, he always worried about her working nights. He knew she was working hard and training to be a Store Manager, so he would never do anything to discourage her. "Ok Jessica, I guessed we'll celebrate another time."

"Thanks for understanding Dad." She replied.

Jessica's had been working at the department store at the Key Mall for nearly two years. She loved her job for most of the year, but it could be very stressful during the Christmas Season. She normally worked a forty-hour week, which included working two nights.

When she arrived for work the store manager informed her that she would be ringing register tonight.

After several hours and looking at her watch for the third time, she realized it was only ten forty-five. She had been busy all evening and usually the time quickly passed-by when she rang register, but tonight it seemed to be dragging.

Glancing back at the ten-people standing in line, she suddenly got a content look on her face when she saw him, *finally, a good-looking guy's coming through my line.* The only thing that she really liked about ringing register was that every now and then she'd meet a hot guy. When he noticed Jessica looking towards him, he gave her a smile and a playful glint, which she promptly returned.

He finally made his way to the front of the line and was holding three oxford shirts with three pair of dress pants. They made small talk flirting back and forth and when she handed him the change, she noticed that he was wearing a wedding band, o*f course you might know it; all the good ones are taken*, she thought. As he stuffed the bills into his wallet Jessica noticed a small tattoo of a cross on his left wrist.

The stranger continued to flirt with Jessica, but she was already over it, the wedding band had completely turned her off. He thanked her, turned and strolled away from the register heading towards the nearest exit. As he passed through the big glass doors, he wiped the sweat from his forehead and whispered under his breath, "I'm going to fuck her tonight."

CHAPTER 17

HIS DARK PASSENGER had returned and this time it was for Jessica. He often wonders, *what compels him to commit this cunning, primitively brutal crime, the pre-empting of another person's body for the gratification of his own needs. He was a sexually troubled youngster who was abused as a child and grew up feeling angry, unwilling or unable to extend compassion. Had this caused him to want to punish, humiliate, dominate, overpower and control women? Yes!*

He hadn't done anything like this in a long time and he knew if he started up again, it would be difficult to stop. A few years ago, when he lived in Virginia, he had raped two girls and gotten away with it. When he attempted to rape a third girl he was nearly caught and swore he would never do it again. His time had run out in Virginia and he knew he had to move on before he made a serious mistake. That's when he and his wife move to Frederick Maryland.

He sat outside of the department store and waited for Jessica to get off work. She was a good-looking brunette and he thought he saw her coming through the big glass doors several times, but it wasn't her. They were all turning out to be false alarms and he was growing impatient.

It was nearly twelve-thirty when she finally exited the store carrying a bag in her left hand and her purse over her right shoulder. He could feel his pulse rate rising and the blood rushing to his head and other places. He was getting an erection just watching her walk across the parking lot. She was beautiful, and it was as if she was a model walking the runway on display just for him.

As she headed towards her car his mind was racing back and forth, *Should I run over to her car and fuck her right here in the parking lot? No, that's too dangerous, the smart thing would be for me to follow her a couple of days and figure out her routine.* He was trying hard to talk himself out of what he wanted to do to Jessica. On second thought, *she really wants it after all she started flirting with me first.*

Jessica got into her car, started it and pulled out of the parking lot. He waited until she had gotten out of the lot before starting his car. There was no need to rush he could see the car sitting at the light near the mall exit. The light changed, and she turned out of the mall merging on to the highway. He took off across the parking lot trying not to get too far behind.

He would need to hurry to make it through the mall exit while the light was still green.

Behind her now on the highway, he was following at a safe distance when she veered off to the right onto route twenty-six. There wasn't much traffic on the highway at this time of night and he could see her car up ahead.

She turned into the Meadows Subdivision and he followed as she weaved her way through to the last section where they had just started to build. Suddenly, she turned right into a large parking lot and he quickly stopped behind a clump of trees, killed the lights and jumped out of his car.

Hiking through the tree line, he stopped at the edge and watched as she entered the end unit. He noticed there weren't any other cars in the parking lot. There was a total of seven townhouses, and it appeared that she was the first one to move in, *could he possibly be that lucky, he couldn't be sure, but he was going for it, he couldn't resist.* This wasn't his normal routine, he usually liked to stalk his victims for a few days and develop a plan that would include when and where he was going to rape them.

He watched the front of her townhome and saw the lights go out on the first floor and a few minutes later the lights came on upstairs. There were no blinds or drapes at the windows, and he had a perfect sightline straight into Jessica's bedroom. She began to unbutton her white blouse that he had been staring down earlier. Unsnapping her bra, she glided it down over her arms, dropping it. Unzipping her skirt from the side, she let it fall to the floor and stepped out of it. Slowly, she pulled her white-laced panties down over her hips and he could barely stand it. She was putting on a show just for him and judging from the bulge in his pants, it was working.

Beautiful body, long brown hair and nice perky little breasts, just my type, he thought.

She glided a pink nightgown over her head and slowly let it drop. It seemed to hang up on the nipples of her perfectly shaped breasts. She tugged a little and slowly pulled it down over her beautiful hips. "Damn even that was tantalizing." He whispered. The question is, *what's the plan? How am I going to get inside that townhouse? Should I pick the lock on the front door, ring the doorbell and push my way in, or maybe just kick in the front door.*

CHAPTER 18

HE WAS SWEATING PROFUSELY as he came out of the tree line and hurry through the tall field of grass. When he was directly in front of Jessica's townhouse, he darted across the street towards the stairs. He was within fifty feet of the front porch and still wasn't sure how he was going to get inside.

Slipping a mask down over his head he hit the first step and in two leaps, he was up on the porch landing. Pulling on his rubber gloves, he snaps them like a surgeon. He placed his left hand over the peephole and rang the doorbell with his right.

After a few minutes, there was a scuffling sound of movement coming from inside the townhouse. He hoped that his twenty minutes of surveillance was correct, and Jessica was alone.

She slowly approached the door in a panic not knowing exactly what to do and asked, "Who is it?"

She was nervous and scared knowing no one should be knocking on her door at this time of night, after all she just moved in today. She tried looking through the peephole but couldn't see anything. "This is the Police, open up, we have a situation," he said.

"Who is it?" she repeated and tried to look out the peephole again but couldn't see a thing.

"Open up," he repeated.

"Show me your badge."

"Open the door so I can show it to you."

She unlocked the door and opened it about six inches leaving the chain hooked. Looking down, she saw what appeared to be a gold badge and inched the door open a little further. Just then he kicked the door open snapping the chain. He turned back towards the door swinging it shut and locked it. Pointing a gun at her he barked, "if you cooperate, I won't hurt you, but if you scream, I'll kill you."

"What the fuck do you want? I don't have any money, get out."

"I told you to keep quiet and I'm not here for your money, I'm here for you, take off that fucking nightgown."

"Please don't do this" she mumbled and began shaking her head back and forth as the tears were streaming down her face.

"I said, take it off or I will blow your fucking head off."

She slowly pulled the nightgown up past her hips then up over her breasts and dropped it to the floor. He began pulling pillows from the couch and threw them on the floor in a straight line. "Lay down on the pillows."

"Please, I beg you, don't do this, just leave me alone and I'll never tell anyone about this, it never happened."

"I told you to get the fuck down on those pillows now" he said and shoved her. Jessica fell backwards onto the pillows and before she realized what was happening, he was on top of her kissing her mouth and she felt sick, his breath stunk like stale cigarettes.

She fought and squirmed trying to fight him off, until he punched her in the face. Her lip was bleeding but he didn't seem to care. He just kept doing what he was doing. Suddenly, he jerked away from her and pulled a condom from his coat pocket. He bit off the end of the packet and quickly put on the condom. From that point on Jessica had given up and didn't try to fight back. She was too scared and just wanted it to be over.

He was on top of her again and inside her in an instant. He was hurting her, and she wanted to scream but now he had his right hand covering her mouth and all she could do was whimper. The taste of the rubber glove in her mouth was sickening and she was afraid she was going to throw up and choke on her own vomit. Her only thought was, *I've never felt more degraded.*

When he finished, he stood up and stared down at her for a few seconds still lying on the pillows. Pulling a brown paper bag from his pocket, he took off the condom and the rubber gloves dropping them inside the bag. He picked up the condom wrapper, dropped it in the bag then folded up the bag and put it inside his pocket.

Stooping down, he leaned over towards Jessica ear and whispered, "Let this be our little secret, if you ever tell anyone, I will come back here and kill you, do you understand?"

She nodded her head up and down as if to say yes. He turned and calmly saunters towards the front door. Opening the door, he looked both ways to make sure no one was around and stepped out onto the front porch pulling the door shut.

Jerking off the mask, he was down the steps in two leaps and quickly took off across the street into the tall grass. He made a right turn into the tree line and came out of the woods on the other side. Jumping into his car he made a U turn and headed home.

Once he had reached the main highway he glanced up into the rearview mirror on the front windshield and smirked back at himself. It was, as if he was confirming some sort of great accomplishment, that he had just raped another beautiful young woman and gotten away with it. When he gotten married, he had hoped that he might have a chance to be human, but his dark passenger is always letting him know it's still there and still alive.

Jessica lay on the pillows crying and wondering, *why did this happen to me, what could I have possibly done to deserve this? I need to pull myself together and call the police. I think I know him, I recognize that voice, but where from?*

Suddenly, it came to her and hit her like a ton of bricks. When he pulled off the rubber gloves, she had noticed a small tattoo of a cross on his left wrist and his wedding band. It was the guy from the store that she had been flirting with earlier tonight, *was this fault, did I lead him on.*

She pulled herself up from the couch pillows, grabbed her pink nightgown and quickly put it on. Picking up the phone she called the police.

The dispatcher said, "Frederick Police Department, how can I help?"

"I've been raped."

"Is the rapist gone?

"Yes, he's gone, please send help as soon as possible, I'm all alone and I'm afraid he might come back.

"There is a female officer on the way, please stay on the line until she arrives."

"Ok, Jessica mumbled.

CHAPTER 19

JESSICA COULD HEAR a siren off at a distance and it seemed to be getting louder and louder. She was on the phone with the Frederick Police Department who had asked her to provide her name and some additional information.

Suddenly, there was a loud knock on the door and a female's voice said, "Police, open up."

Fear and shock abruptly came over her, it was exactly what the rapist had said just before he busted open her front door. Slowly, she made her way towards the door and glared out the peephole. There were two uniformed police officers standing on her front porch. Slowly, she swung the door open and the female officer said in a profound voice, "are you Jessica Green?"

"Yes," she said wiping away the mascara that had ran down her cheeks.

"This is my partner Officer Evan Howell and I'm Officer Sherry Gross, may we come in?"

"Yes," Jessica replied moving to the side.

Officer Gross stepped inside the townhouse and noticed the couch pillows lying on the floor and asked, "is that where it happen?"

"Yes," Jessica replied, as tears began to trickle down her cheeks.

Pulling out a notepad Officer Gross said, I'm sorry but I need to get a short statement from you right away, do you think you can do that?

"I'll try," Jessica said and spent the next several minutes describing the horror that she had gone through.

A short time later, the crime scene investigators had arrived from the Maryland State Police and began to process the crime scene. A sketch artist sat at the kitchen table with Jessica and did a composite drawing of the assailant.

Officer Gross approached Jessica and explained, "I need to take you to Frederick Memorial Hospital to be examined. They'll be looking for hair and fiber from the rapist. Please understand this could lead to the capture of the man who did this to you."

"Ok, thanks." Jessica replied.

Officer Gross escorted Jessica outside to where she had parked her car, drove to the hospital and waited in the lobby while the doctor did a rape kit examination.

Thirty minutes later the doctor came out of the examination room and approached Officer Gross, "you can see Jessica now. There's evidence that she was raped, I'll have a full report for you tomorrow morning. The only hair or fiber discovered was from Jessica nothing from the attacker."

"What about semen?" Officer Gross asked.

"There wasn't any."

Officer Gross strolled down the hallway towards Jessica room, dreading the conversation she was about to have.

Entering the examination room, she approached Jessica and said, "Sorry to do this Jessica but I need to ask you a few more questions."

"Ok, but just a few I got to get out of here.

"I understand, and I'll try to be brief, was your attacker wearing a condom?

"Yes, he wore a condom, rubber gloves and a mask."

"What happen to the condom?"

"It was weird, he pulled a brown paper bag out of his coat pocket, dropped the condom and rubber gloves inside, then folded it up and stuck it in his pocket."

"Did you notice if he had any distinguishing marks or tattoos?"

"Yes, as a matter of fact when he was taking off the rubber gloves, I saw a small tattoo of a cross on his left wrist."

"Do you think you might know the guy who did this?"

"Well, he was wearing a mask, but I think I waited on him at work earlier tonight, he must have followed me home. I should have never flirted with him, this is all my fault."

"This is not your fault Jessica; this guy is a sick bastard." Officer Gross alleged.

Jessica began to cry again and started to mumble, "he had a gun and I thought he was going to kill me so at some point I stopped fighting, I just wanted it to be over."

"That's all for now but the detectives from FPD will follow-up with you in a day or two." Officer Gross explained.

Officer Gross didn't want to push Jessica any further she was in a very fragile state. She handed Jessica her card and asked her to give her a call if she remembered anything else. Jessica's Mother and Father enter the room and Officer Gross exited.

CHAPTER 20

March 1, 1991

THE RAPIST CAME HOME from work around five o'clock and his wife Barbara was standing inside the front door waiting for him to enter. "I have some great news, we're pregnant."

"Are you sure?" he asked. They'd been trying unsuccessfully to have a baby for a few years so this was exhilarating news.

"Yes, Doctor More confirmed it this morning."

Extremely happy, he hugged and kissed her, "we need to go out and celebrate I'll take you to Clyde's for dinner"

Clyde's is located at Eveready Square, sort of fancy and one of the most expensive restaurants in town. "We can't afford that," Barbara replied.

"Don't worry about it, this is a special occasion and we should celebrate, I'll call and make the reservations."

"Ok, if you think we can swing it," Barbara replied as she hurried off yelling over her shoulder.

Barbara got out of the shower and stood naked in front of the mirror admiring how good she looked. She rubbed her stomach but hadn't really started to show her pregnancy yet. To say that she was beautiful was and understatement. Her hair was a rich shade of mahogany and flowed in waves to adorn her glowing, exotic porcelain-like skin. Her eyes, framed by long lashes, were a chocolate brown with tones of amber in them.

Barbara grabbed her favorite black dress from the bedroom closet and her sexiest black-laced bra and underwear from a drawer. Approaching the bed, she carefully laid them out thinking *I'm going to make this a night for him to remember.*

Arriving in front the restaurant at seven forty-five, Barbara's husband drifted to a stop. There was an oval red canopy coming off the building with red indoor-outdoor carpet leading to the front door. A valet opened Barbara's door and took her hand helping her from the vehicle. Her husband hooked her arm and escorted her up the red carpet and just for a moment she felt, *like a real movie star.*

Entering the restaurant, they approached the hostess and Barbara's husband said, "We have reservation for eight p.m."

"What name," the hostess asked.

"That's it right there," he replied pointing to their name listed in the reservation book lying on the podium.

"Yes, of course, your table is ready, please follow me," the hostess replied and lead them to a round table for two near the back of the restaurant. It was dimly lit and romantic with a candle in the center of the table. The table was covered with a white linen tablecloth and fancy triangle shape beige napkins.

Barbara's husband leaned over kissing her on the lips and her feelings at that moment were indescribable. The kiss had been long, wet and passionate. It was a passion that he hadn't shared for a long time. Something had disappeared over the past few years, sure, there was sex, but it seemed more like anger at times instead of passion.

A waitress suddenly approached the table and said, "hi I'm Gina and I'll be taking care of you this evening."

"We would like to start off with a bottle of wine, we're celebrating," Barbara's husband explained.

"Sure, I understand," Gina said and pointed out the restaurant's top three wines. Barbara picked a white and Gina headed off towards the bar to retrieve it. As she was walking away Barbara's husband couldn't help but admiring how beautiful she was and thought, *she has a great body, long brown hair, just my type.*

The evening progressed, and Barbara thanked her husband and explained that, this was the nicest restaurant she'd ever been to. The food was great, and the waitress gave them excellent service. He agreed with everything she had said and made it a point to give the waitress a very nice tip. They stood-up to leave the restaurant and he let his wife walk out one step ahead of him, because he wanted to glance back and take one last look at Gina.

Driving home, Barbara's husband stopped the car at the corner liquor store and bought a bottle of her favorite wine. When they got home, he headed to the kitchen to open the wine and get some glasses. Barbara yelled to him, "I'll be upstairs waiting for you."

As she began climbing the stairs, she dropped one of her black high heel slippers on the first step and another on the third step. On the sixth step she dropped her black stockings and in the upstairs hallway she dropped her short black dress.

A few minutes later he saw the trail of clothes that she was leaving behind, he could feel the excitement building and began climbing the stairs two at a time.

When he reached the bedroom, Barbara's bra was hanging on the doorknob and her panties were lying on the floor in front of the bed. She was lying on the bed completely naked, and he couldn't help thinking, *it's been a long time since she's turned me on this much.*

He ripped off his clothes and climbed into bed next to her. Grabbing her face between his hands, he forced her to look up into his, determined eyes. He kissed her, violently, and then his tongue was in her mouth. Desire exploded throughout her body, and she's kissing him back, matching his fervor. He groans, a low sexy sound in the back of his throat that reverberates through her, and his hand moves down her body to the top of her thigh, his fingers digging into her flesh. Pulling him tight against her, trying to control the reaction in her body. She feels stiflingly hot, flustered, and her legs are like jelly as dark desire courses through her. She wants him. He is so tantalizingly close, and his scent is intoxicating.

"Tell me what you want," his eyes smolder and his lips part as he takes quick shallow breaths.

"Kiss me," she whispered.

"Where?"

"You know where."

"Where?"

She quickly points to the apex of her thighs, and he grins. She closed her eyes, mortified, but at the same time aroused.

"With pleasure," he chuckles. He kisses her unleashing his tongue, his joy-inspiring expert tongue. She groans and brushes her hands through his hair. He doesn't stop, his tongue circling her clitoris, driving her insane, on and on, around and around.

"I want you inside me now," she gasps.

"Are you sure?"

"Please." She pleads staring down at him in frantic need.

He slowly crawls up over her, kissing her as he goes. He kisses each of her breasts and teases her nipples in turn, while she groans and writhes beneath him, and he doesn't stop. Gazing down at her, he pushes her legs apart with his hand and moves so that he's hovering above her. Without taking his eyes off hers, he sinks into her at a deliciously slow pace.

She closed her eyes, relishing the fullness, the exquisite feeling of his possession, instinctively tilting her pelvis up to meet him, to join him, groaning loudly. He eases back and very slowly fills her again.

Her fingers find their way into his unruly hair, and he oh-so-slowly moves in and out again.

"Faster, please…faster," she cried out.

He gazes down at her in triumph and kisses her hard, then really starts to move-*a punishing, relentless…oh fuck-and* she knows she won't be long. He sets a pounding rhythm. She starts to quicken, her legs tensing beneath him.

"Come on, baby," he gasps. "Give it to me."

His words were her undoing, and she explodes, magnificently, mind-numbingly, into a million pieces around him, and he follows, calling out her name.

"Barbara! Oh fuck, Barbara!" He collapses on top of her, his head buried in her neck.

CHAPTER 21

MY DARK PASSENGER is what I call my need to rape. It's been with me ever since college pulling the strings running the show, I'm its puppet. A few days had passed and no matter how hard the rapist tried, he couldn't stop thinking about Gina,

He decided to go to Clyde's for lunch hoping that she would be working, because he simply had to see her again. He entered the restaurant and saw her across the room waiting on a customer. She was radiant, with her long brown hair that seem to be gleaming from to overhead lights. He approached the hostess and asked, "May I please be seated in Gina's Section?"

"Of course, please follow me," she replied.

Gina glanced over and saw him being seated and remembered him from the big tip that he had left her a few nights ago. She approached his table and said, "Hello, will your wife be joining you today?

"No, she's at home, I wasn't really sure you'd remember me," he replied.

"Sure, I remember you, I enjoyed waiting on you guys the other night, you were celebrating a special occasion, right."

"That's right, my wife just found out that she's having a baby."

"Sure, I remember, congratulations, what can I get you to drink?"

"I'll take a diet coke, please."

"Be right back," she replied.

The restaurant wasn't too busy, so they found time to talk, which was good, because his real motive was to find out as much as he could about Gina. He discovered that her full name was Gina Cooper and she was currently working at the restaurant part time and attending Frederick Community College at night. He also learned that she was still living with her parents.

"Gina approached his table for the fifth time and asked, "Can I get you another drink?"

Glancing at his watch he realized he had already stretched his lunch into nearly two hours talking and flirting with Gina "It's been great talking to you, but I've really need to get back to work, I'll take my check."

"Sure," she responded and began clearing the table.

Dropping a napkin on the floor, she bent over to pick it up. Staring at her cure butt he noticed a tattoo on her back when her blouse rose up.

"Nice tattoo," he said smiling as she stood up.

"You mean my Tramp Stamp" she replied and they both laughed.

"I wouldn't call it that, in fact I think it's pretty sexy."

"Thanks, I like yours too," she replied pointing to the little cross located on his left wrist.

"I got that when I was about twelve."

"Didn't your parents get upset?"

"A little, but it was too late to do anything about it.

"I guess so, I'll be right back with your check."

A few minutes late Gina returned with his check and said, "thanks for coming in today, I hope you come back and see us real soon."

"I'm sure I will, thanks," he said as he took the check to sign leaving her another nice tip.

Exiting the restaurant, he climbed into his car reflecting on what had just happened and thought, *the more I talked to her, the more I'm intrigued. It's been nearly three months since my last rape, but unfortunately my dark passenger is starting to seize my mind and body again. I'm like an alcoholic trying to resist that first drink after being sober for a while. I see a beautiful girl, like Gina Cooper and realize that I must have her.*

CHAPTER 22

THE RAPIST HAD BEEN STALKING Gina for several weeks and appreciated the fact that she was a creature of habit. When she gets off work, she always stops at seven-eleven for a coffee and then drives straight to Frederick Community College (FCC) for her evening classes.

He sat in his car waiting for her to exit the building after her class, which ended at 10:00 p.m. It was already 10:15 and she was normally out by now, *could something be wrong?* Students were exiting left and right, and the parking lot was nearly empty. Finally, at 10:45 Gina exited through the double doors of the classroom building walking alone. Usually, when she came out, she was with other students, but not tonight, *could this be my night.*

The classroom building was nearly a quarter mile away from the parking lot. There was a long sidewalk leading from the classrooms up past the gym and tennis courts to the parking lot. Cautiously looking around, the rapist didn't see anyone. Looking back towards Gina, she had distanced herself a little way from the classroom building.

Jumping out of his car, he rushed across the parking lot disappearing in-between the tennis courts and the east end of the gym. His plan was to circle around the gym and double back to approach Gina from behind.

He began to sweat as he felt a delightful rush of excitement coming over him. Peaking around the corner, he didn't see her, *Perfect "maybe"*, he knew if she got past the east end of the gym and the tennis courts it would be too late and his plan wouldn't work. He jogged down along the west end of the gym reaching the front corner and stopped. He looked both ways to see if anyone else was coming from the classrooms or the parking lot and didn't see anyone.

Looking around the front corner of the gym he saw Gina passing the double glass entrance doors in the center of the building. Turning the corner, he began walking up the sidewalk in front of the gym quickly increasing his speed. He was closing in on her trying to time everything just perfect. Taking one last look back and then looking up ahead to the parking lot, there was no one else around *great, tonight the night.* Pulling a mask from his pocket, he swiftly heaved it down over his face.

He began to jog more rapidly catching up with her and shoved his gun into the small of her back. Grabbing the neckline of her dress he pushed her and said, "Don't make a sound or I blow your fucking head off."

When they reached the east corner of the gym, he pushed her to the side of the building between the gym and the tennis courts. Finally reaching the end of the building he pulled her behind it where no one could see or hear them from the parking lot or the classroom building.

Gina tried fighting and began to pull away when the rapist punched her in the face knocking her to the ground. He pointed his gun towards her and said, "I told you not to make a fucking sound and stop fighting me."

Tears began to run down Gina face, and she said, "please don't hurt me, you don't have to do this, just walk away and I promise I'll never tell anyone."

"I told you to shut the fuck up," he said as he lowered himself down and ripped her dress from her shoulders exposing her bra. Grabbing the bra, he yang it up over her breasts scratching her. His hands move up to her breasts, and he palms them both, tugging on her nipples. She groaned in pain and tossed her head from side to side. She could smell the stench of cigarettes on his clothes and it was making her sick. He kisses, bites her ear and she try to scream, but he places his hand over her mouth, she can taste the rubber gloves and it's nauseating.

Hovering over her, he slides on a condom, and then he's inside her hard and fast. "Oh yes! You like that don't you?" he groans as he slams into her and begins a punishing rhythm. He nuzzles her neck, biting down, as he flexes his hips and picks up speed. He snakes one hand around her waist and grasps her hip and pushes into her harder, making her cry out again. Finally, he empties himself inside her and was finished. What now she wondered, *is he going to kill me?*

Standing up, he removed a brown paper bag from his pocket and dropped the used condom and rubber gloves inside. Carefully folding up the bag, he stuffed it back inside his coat pocket. She was lying on the ground watching him closely and praying he wasn't going to kill her. Suddenly, she noticed the small tattoo of a cross on his left wrist and quickly turned her head. She couldn't let him know that she recognized him, or he would kill her for sure.

Could this really be the same guy who brought his wife to Clyde's to celebrate and came back a few days later it can't be, he was so nice to me.

The rapist took one last look at how beautiful Gina was lying on the ground sobbing. Squatting down, he whispered into her ear, "this is going to be our little secret, don't get up for ten minutes or I'll kill you, understand." She tried to speak, but there was no sound, so she just nodded her head, hoping that would be enough.

He stood up, turned away from Gina and began to hurry off towards the east corner of the gym. Turning the corner, he ripped off his mask and stuffed it inside his coat pocket. Reaching his car, he quickly unlocked it, climbed in and took off. He spun the wheels as he exited the parking lot and headed home.

Glancing into the rearview mirror, the serious look on his face suddenly turned into an obnoxious smirk, signifying he had gotten away with another rape. *We all make rules for ourselves, rules that help define who we are, then we break the rules and risk losing ourselves.*

Gina stayed on the ground for what she believed to be ten minutes. She wasn't sure if she was too afraid to move or simply couldn't. When she finally tried to get up every bone in her body was aching, he had really hurt her physical and mentally. She pulled her bra down and raised her dress back over her shoulders.

Struggling to get to her feet, she gathered up her books and her purse. Stumbling from behind the building, she had no idea where she was going. Turning the corner of the building she rambled down the sidewalk in front of the gym. When she reached the center of the building, she peered through the double glass doors and could see some guys playing basketball.

Pulling one of the doors open she step inside and staggered across the basketball court towards the players. One of the players noticed her coming towards them with a bloody face and a torn dress.

He dropped the basketball and ran towards her yelling, "what's wrong?"

"I've been raped," she said but no sound came from her mouth and suddenly she collapsed.

The basketball player turned to his friends and yelled, "Call the police and ambulance."

CHAPTER 23

THE DISPATCHER ANSWERED the phone, "Frederick Police Department, what's your emergency?"

"Hello this is John Dean, please send an ambulance and the police to the gym at Frederick Community College as soon as possible."

"Calm down, what's going on?" the dispatcher inquired.

"We think someone's been raped, we were playing basketball at the gym and a girl staggered in and clasped in front of us. Her clothes are torn, I think she's been beaten, there's blood on her face."

"Officers are on the way and I'll call and ambulance, they should be there in a few minutes."

Approximately five minutes later two paramedics dress in blue uniforms came bursting through the double glass doors pushing a gurney with a big red equipment bag on top. They saw the young men gathered around the woman lying on the floor and rush over. She was awake but appeared to be mentally confused and disorientated. The paramedics loaded her onto the gurney and were preparing to take her to the hospital. She was trembling and had vomited down the front of her dress.

Two police officers entered the gym and Officer Sherry Gross asked the paramedics, "Can we ask her a few questions?"

"No, she's in shock and can't speak."

"Ok, we'll try again later at the hospital," Officer Gross replied.

"Officer Evan Howell began to question the young men, "Can anyone tell me what happen here?"

One of the young men began to speak, "we were playing basketball and I heard someone open the glass doors over there. When I look over, she was stumbling towards us with blood on her face and I ran towards her? She tried to say something, but no sound came out and then she just collapsed."

"Is there anyone else in the gym beside you six guys?" Officer Gross asked.

"No, just us playing basketball and whatever happened to her, happened outside the gym, maybe a car or something."

"There's only one car in the parking lot and it's a 57 Chevy," Officer Howell replied.

"That's my car," John replied.

Another kid spoke-up, "We've all been right here on the court for at least an hour."

"We need to have our forensics' team check out the car. Do we have your permission, or do we need to get a search warrant?" Officer Gross asked.

"Go ahead and check it out, I got nothing to hide," John replied.

Other police officers were arriving, and Officer Gross asked them to do a sweep around the outside of the buildings to look for any possible evidence, "I think from the looks of her she may have been raped."

Thirty minutes later an officer reported that he had found a small piece of silver wrapping behind the gym. He believed that it could be part of a condom wrapper. Also, the grass was smash down in that area.

The forensics team had arrived and began examining the car, Officer Howell and Officer Gross excused themselves and drove to the hospital. Approaching the nurse's station Officer Gross said, "we're here to interview Gina Cooper who was brought in less than an hour ago."

"I'm afraid you won't be able to interview her, she's still in shock and not able to speak," the nurse explained.

"Is that normal," Officer Howell asked.

"It's important that we recognize that people respond differently to trauma, but let me page the doctor, she may be able to provide you with more information," the nurse responded.

A few minutes later a doctor approached the nurse's station and introduced herself, "Hi I'm Doctor Sara Moore."

"Please to meet you Doctor Moore, I'm Officer Gross and this is my partner Officer Howell."

"Can you confirm that the victim was raped?" Officer Howell asked.

"Yes, we did a rape kit examination and can confirmed that's she was raped, but unfortunately, we didn't find any semen, hair or fiber from the assailant."

"Well can you explain her not being able to talk?" Officer Gross asked.

"Rape Trauma Syndrome (RTS) is the medical term given to the response that some survivors get after being raped.

RTS is the natural response of a psychologically healthy person's reaction to the trauma of getting raped."

So, if I understand what you're saying Doctor, at some point she will be able to speak again? Officer Howell asked.

"Yes, it could be a day, a week or several months, it depends on the induvial, Doctor more explained.

"Ok, thanks for the information Doc," Officer Gross replied.

The two police officers exited the hospital and Officer Howell turned to Officer Gross and asked, "Well what now partner?"

"Let's go to HQ and write-up our report and we'll turn the case file over to the Detectives in the morning, so they can follow-up. There's not much more we can do," Officer Gross explained.

"Sounds like a plan partner." Officer Howell responded as they strolled off towards their patrol car.

CHAPTER 24

April 26, 1991

NICKOLAS BURNS IS OVER six feet tall and weighs 180 pounds. He has a thin face with gray hair, and he's been told that his adam's apple sticks out too far. His friends often tell him, that he reminds them of Clint Eastwood and calls him "Dirty Harry" for laughs.

Nick's wife Sandy is a lawyer who stands around five ten, without the three-inch heels that she loves so much. She has golden blonde hair and a sculpted figure, she has managed to preserve since her college days. They have two children, a daughter Mandy who just turned eighteen and a son Jerry who is sixteen.

Nick and Sandy began dating two weeks after they met in their senior year of high school. They both attended Louisiana State and continue to date throughout their college years. After graduating from College Sandy found a job as an associate lawyer working for the District Attorney in Chicago Illinois. Nick took a job at a local restaurant washing dishes, worked his way up to become a waiter and eventually Assistant Manager.

One day while reading the newspaper, Nick noticed an advertisement for new recruits with the Chicago Police Department (CPD). To qualify you needed to complete an eight-week training course at the Police Officer's Training Academy. If you were able to make it through the academy you would be eligible to join the CPD.

Nick discussed it with Sandy, and she supported him one hundred percent, but told him the final decision was his. He decided to give it a try and completed the training at the top of his class. CPD offered him a position as a rookie patrolman and he accepted it.

After two years as a beat cop Nick decided to take the Detective's Exam and surprised everyone when he passed it on the first try. Subsequently, he had to find an open position in one of the ten precincts. A month later, there was an opening located in the ninth precinct. He applied for it and was offered a Detective 1st grade position working in the Special Cold Cases Unit (SCCU). The SCCUs primary function was to worked murder cases that weren't solved within the first year.

Nick enjoyed working cold cases because he felt like the homicide detectives had already done most of the legwork.

Sometimes, a little different prospective was all it took to solve an old case. When he was assigned a case, he was relentless, often not sleeping for days until it was solved.

Eventually, he transferred to the Major Crimes Homicide Unit, worked his way through the ranks and after seven years became the Chief of Police. It was very unusual, for anyone to progress through the ranks so rapidly, but in the past five years prior to becoming the Chief, he had solved more murder cases than any Detective in the history of CPD.

Sandy was very surprised, but happy when Nick came home from work one day and told her he was ready to retire after twenty-one years. He felt burned out and thought the time had come for them to move on. Nick began searching for a new job and Sandy had asked him to try and find something other than law enforcement. But that was all he knew, unless he went back to washing dishes and that wasn't going to happen.

After several months and many applications, he decided to take a position as the new Chief of Police in Frederick Maryland. He had received some better offers, but for him it wasn't about the money he wanted to get away from the murder and mayhem of the big city. He was looking for a small-town atmosphere and Frederick was a very small town compared to Chicago.

A few weeks prior to Nick's start date the family traveled to Frederick to look for a new home. They had previously contacted a realtor and asked her to schedule some viewings. At the end of the day they agreed on the first house that they'd looked at and made an offer. The house was located on Madison Street and was a beautiful two story in the middle of the block. The living room had gorgeous beige carpet and a stone fireplace. The large kitchen had oak cabinets and on the second floor there were four bedrooms, the Master bedroom, a bedroom for each of the kids and Nick had decided to convert the fourth bedroom into a home office, with Sandy's permission, of course.

CHAPTER 25

June 3rd, 1991

THE DREADED ALARM clock began to ring at six a.m. and Nick jumped out of bed turning it off. Anxious to get his day started, he hurried off to get a shower. He wanted to be at work by seven to meet his new employees.

Kissing Sandy good-bye at the front door, he smiled as he climbed into the car and rushed off towards his new job as Chief of Police for FPD. Parking across the street from the HQ building located on North Market Street, he noticed that the building was in very bad disrepair, *there goes my budget*, he thought.

Entering the building, it felt like he'd stepped back in time twenty years. The paint was literally peeling off the walls and the hardwood creaked as he walked across the old wooden floors. The oak desks in the squad room were facing each other in pairs of two and appeared to be antiques.

A large black man rambled towards Nick, held out his hand and introduced himself, "Hello Chief, I'm Detective Dominick Thomas."

Nick shook his hand and replied, "Please to meet you Detective."

Detective Thomas turned and pointed to his partner who was trailing along behind, "This is my partner, Duke Wayne, we're your detective's here at FPD."

'Just the two of you?" Nick asked, trying not to reveal his disappointment, *I had sixty-one Detectives under my command in Chicago, it looks like I'm going to have two here in Frederick and one's name is Duke Wayne no less.*

Detective Thomas could sense Chief Burns disappointment and followed-up, "Chief, we also have ninety-one uniformed officers and the Sheriff's Department has eighty-three deputies. Not to mention the Maryland State Police, who have a staff of thirty-five. All of our branches have a very close working relationship."

"Thanks for the information detective, I'd like to meet with you in my office at two o'clock this afternoon. I'll need you to brief me on the cases you are currently working and the three unsolved murder cases you have on the books."

"Why do you want briefed on the unsolved cases? There were intense investigations by the FPD, MSP and the FBI on those cases and they were never solved. What makes you think we can solve them?" Detective Wayne asked.

"I'm not certain we can Detective, but it wouldn't hurt to take a fresh look. We'll discuss it further at our two o'clock. Meeting," Chief Burns replied.

The new Chief turned and ambled off towards his office and settled into his big leather chair. He pulled a pen from his shirt pocket and began filling out papers from the personnel package HR had given him. After a couple of hours, he was so tired that he could barely hold his head up, *time to take a break,* he thought.

Leaning back in his chair, he thought, *what the hell am I doing here?* Glancing around his new office he noticed there was a large bookshelf with a complete set of law books, *impressive*, he thought. There was no overhead lighting just a floor lamp and an ugly green desk light sitting on the edge of his desk. The desk was made of oak and must have been at least two hundred years old. He thought it would be a beautiful antique with some furniture polish and elbow grease. There was a glass entry door to his office and the Town Council had his name painted on it.

Looking at his watch he couldn't believe it was nearly lunchtime. Jumping up from his desk, he hurried towards the door he wanted to make sure he'd be back in plenty of time for his 2:00 o'clock meeting. He climbed into his car, drove to a sub shop that he'd heard about from one of the uniforms and was back at the office by one-thirty.

Opening the top drawer of his antique desk, he pulled out a yellow notepad. Although he wanted to know exactly what the detectives were working on, he was much more interested in hearing about the three cold cases. A friend, Jim Hilliard had told him about the cases a few months ago. Jim had been with the FPD for twelve years and decided to move to Chicago. He joined the CPD and one night they were sitting around having a few beers when he told Chief Burns about the unsolved murders.

The two detectives arrived together, knocked on Chief Burns open office door and entered. The chief invited them to have a seat and begin briefing him on their current caseload. "Chief we are working on four street robberies, one assault and two rape cases.

We have a suspect for the street robberies and some uniforms are assigned to keep an eye on him, the plan is to catch him in the act. For the aggravated assault, we made an arrest two days ago. A husband beat-up his ex-wife bad in fact, put her in the hospital. It turns out that they had just gone through a nasty divorce and a big custody battle. The judge had given the wife everything and her husband decided to make her pay for it. I suspect he'll be going away for a long time. As for the two rape cases we currently have no suspects."

Detective Wayne spoke up for the first time, "I've been handling the rape cases, but I don't have any leads, so far the rapist hasn't left any forensic evidence behind."

"Do you believe the same person committed both rapes?" Chief Burns asked.

"At this point we don't have any evidence that would connect the two cases," Detective Wayne replied.

"If you need help chasing down information, we can assign some uniforms to interview witnesses for you, just let me know," Chief Burns explained.

"I don't think that'll be necessary," Detective Wayne answered.

"Well, what can you tell me about the three unsolved murder cases?" Chief Burns asked.

"The first case happened August 24, 1982. While out hiking a couple, discovered a trunk located just off the roadway. The trunk contained the body of a white female, approximate age was 18 to 25, with blond hair. The identity of the victim remains a mystery despite investigative efforts by numerous detectives from FPD, MSP and the FBI, the second case happened on August 24, 1986 four years later to the day. The victim was working alone in a store at a local shopping mall and the security guard discovered her body. She was a white female, 19 years of age with blond hair and was positively identified by her parents, and the third unsolved case happened August 24, 1990 four years later. The victim's body was discovered in a wooded area near the Southern Market. She was a white female, 17 years of age with blond hair and was positively identified by her parents." Detective Thomas detailed.

"Do you believe the cases are related somehow?" Chief Burns inquired.

"Yes, we think so, in fact everyone who's ever looked at these cases believe they're connected." Detective Wayne responded.

"What ties them together?" Chief Burns asked.

"There's something we didn't released to the public Chief. All three victims had a set of red lips drawn on the upper portion of their left breasts with lipstick." Detective Thomas replied.

Chief Burns's friend had told him about the unsolved murders that had happed four years apart, but he had never mentioned the red lipstick, *now I'm really intrigued*, he thought.

"Thank you, detectives, for giving me the background on the cold cases, I'm going to reopen them."

"Are you sure you want to do that Chief?" Detective Thomas asked.

"Yes, I'd like to do it not only for the reputation of FPD, but also if we can solve these cases maybe the families can get some closure. I need you to provide me a copy of all the files so I can do an intensive review," Chief burns replied.

"No problem Chief but it's going to take a few days," Detective Thomas explained.

"That's fine, that's all I have for now Detectives."

As the Detectives departed Chief Burns office he couldn't help thinking back to when he was detective in Chicago, *I hated to see a murder happen, but I must admit I loved the adrenalin rush trying to catch a killer. I don't know if we'll discover any new evidence or be able to solve these cases, I only know we need to try.*

CHAPTER 26

THE DESK-SERGEANT entered Chief Burns office after the detectives left, "Chief, I received a request for a meeting with you today from one of our female officer's.

"Do you know what it's about?" Chief Burns asked.

"She didn't say, just that it was important."

"Ok, fine Sergeant, you can have her come-in at three o'clock, can you tell me a little more about her?

"Her name is Faye-Lynn Johnson and she's one of only six female officer's working for FPD. Her rank is a Sergeant and she has been on the force for a little over twelve years. Currently, she's a squad leader and has seven uniform officers assign to her squad."

"Thanks for the information, that'll be all." Chief Burns replied.

At approximately 2:55 there was a knock-on Chief Burns's office door and Officer Faye-Lynn Johnson entered. Chief Burns looked up from his desk and couldn't believe his eyes. Standing before him was the most beautiful black women, he'd ever seen. His first thought was, *what the hell is she doing here? She should be a model or a movie star in fact she could past as Halle Berry twin sister.*

She was wearing a uniform that certainly didn't look like standard issue. The top two buttons of her shirt were unbuttoned showing a little cleavage, which was incredibly sexy. He scanned her body from head to toe and caught himself staring at every tantalizing curve. She had short black hair and was wearing bright red lipstick, which accentuated the beautiful brown tone of her skin. "Hi, I'm Chief Nick Burns, it's a pleasure to meet you."

She reached out, shook his hand and said, "I'm officer Faye-Lynn Johnson, nice to meet you Chief."

"Please have a seat Officer Johnson. By the way, I wanted to mention that I was planning on having one on one meetings with everyone over the next couple of weeks. However, since you requested this meeting, I assumed that you needed to talk to me right away?" Chief Burns explained.

"I'm sorry Chief, I know this is your very first day, but I wanted to speak to you about a personal issue."

"No worries, what can I do for you Officer Johnson?"

"I took the Detectives Exam about a year ago and my goal was to join the detective's squad here at FPD.

Your predecessor, our former Chief led me to believe that if I pass the exam, he would be able to make a spot for me. That never happened, I believe he was just trying to get in my pants and that never happened either."

"Well Officer Johnson, I'm not sure I can be held to the former Chief's promises but let me look into it and I'll get back to you."

Chief Burns and Officer Johnson talked for several more minutes about her current position and duties as a squad leader. She thanked him for taking the time to meet with her and began to leave his office when she suddenly whirled around and said, "By the way Chief, I heard you are re-opening the Lipstick Murders cases."

"The what," he responded.

"The three cold cases that are un-solved."

"Yes, we're going to re-open the cold cases, but I've haven't heard anyone call them that before."

"Sorry Chief, I guess I name them that a long time ago, I've been on the scene of all three murders and saw what the killer did with the lipstick, so I started calling them the lipstick murders."

"Well, I guess that makes sense, thanks for meeting with me Officer Johnson, I'll get back to you on the personal matter as soon as I can. Also give me some time to review the cold case files and we can meet again, I'd like to get your perspective on the cases. By the way do you think the same person or persons killed all three girls?"

"Yes." Officer Johnson responded without hesitation, turned and exited Chief Burns office.

It was 4:15 when Chief Burns began to pack up his brief case with some personnel files to take home and begin reviewing. He made sure to include Officer's Faye-Lynn Johnson's file considering their meeting today. He had to determine if she was qualified to be a Detective for the FPD.

As he leisurely exited the building he thought, *wow, what an interesting first day, can't wait to start working on my new cold cases, the Lipstick Murders.*

CHAPTER 27

CHIEF BURNS SPENT the rest of the week reviewing personnel files and meeting with FPD's uniformed officers. But he couldn't seem to get the three unsolved murder cases off his mind. Late Friday afternoon Detective Thomas knocked on his office door and entered pulling a hand truck with three boxes. "Here's the copies of the case files you requested Chief."

"Thanks Detective, I appreciate it, but I think it's too late to begin reviewing them today. I'll take one home and review it over the weekend." Leaning over, Chief Burns grabbed the box marked August 1982 and exited his office locking the door.

Saturday morning and he was up at 6:00 a.m., he couldn't wait to dig into the case file that he'd brought home. He climbed the stairs to his home office, sat down in his high back leather chair and begins to work. The plan was to review the case files with a fresh set of eyes and give the detectives some leads to follow-up on. He'd previously set up a white board and divided it into three sections, one for each case. He was going to write down what he considered the most important facts for each case and once that's was complete, he'd look for connections.

Removing the lid, he looked inside with no idea of what to expect. The files were mostly reporting from several different investigations but had very little physical evidence. Picking-up the first document, he began to read a report written by, Detective Joe Donavan of the Maryland State Police.

August 25, 1982: *At approximately 7:00 a.m. the Frederick Police Department received a phone call stating that a body had been discovered at the Frederick Watershed. The Frederick Watershed encompasses over 7,000 acres of forestland in western Frederick County. The FPD, Sheriff's Department and the MSP were notified and dispatched to the scene. Officer Faye-Lynn Johnson from FPD was the first to arrive and spoke briefly with the couple that had discovered the body. She proceeded to secure the crime scene with yellow police tape with the assistance of her partner Officer Evan Howell.*

Detective Donavan: *"I arrived at the crime scene at approximately 8:20 a.m., Officer Faye-Lynn Johnson from FPD was the officer-in-charge. I signed into the murder logbook and took possession as ranking officer. Taking command of the crime scene, I did an initial interview with the couple that had discovered the body.*

I then asked Officer Johnson to drive the couple too MSP's HQ, to get their written statements. I canvas the area around the exterior of the trunk and found no evidence. Inside the trunk was a white female, no wallet or purse was discovered, and so the case is officially considered a Jane Doe case.

It appeared from Detective Donavan's report that he was on the scene for approximately 47 minutes. He then left the crime scene and drove to MSPs HQ. The Detective's next log entry was for 11:02, when he began to interview the two witnesses who had discovered the body.

11:02: *According to witnesses Tom and Ellen Ridgeway, they had been out hunting mushrooms at the Frederick Watershed. As they were walking up the road, they noticed a trunk twenty feet from the edge of the road. The trunk was pulled in between two small trees and there were limbs and branches scattered on the top and along the sides. They tried to open the trunk, but discovered it was locked. Tom picked up a rock, hitting it several times before popping it open. Lifting the lid, they discovered a body, at which time Ellen went to a neighbor's house and call the police while Tom stayed with the body.*

Chief Burns had been reading the case files for hours and it was time for a much-needed break. Although the review of the file was going painstaking slow, he knew from his years of experience that this is what it takes to break a murder case. You examine the files again and again until something jumps out at you.

Back at his desk he began reading the forensic report. It seemed short compared to what he'd been used to at CPD. The most interesting thing was, what wasn't there. For instance, there was no blood in the trunk, even though there was a cut on the back of the victim's head. *Three Strands of hair were discovered inside the trunk, two strands matched to victim, but the other one belonged to someone else. A black button and several small pieces of red fiber were recovered but didn't match any of the clothing the victim was wearing. Several fingerprints were discovered on the trunk, one set belonging to Tom Ridgeway, but three others couldn't be identified through the FBI's fingerprint database. Two small pieces of broken glass were recovered, they were tested and determine to be tempered glass and matched the embedded glass on the back of the victim's skull. There was a white unidentified foreign substance on the slacks that the victim was wearing.*

The next document Chief Burns pulled from the box was the pathology report from the Medical Examiner. *The deceased has undergone extensive dental procedures, some of which are consistent with those performed by dental students.*

The dental work included two crowns on her left front teeth, a root canal and several fillings. The spine showed a stress, and a toe that was previously broken, suggesting she may have been a dancer, or physically active. The victim was 5 feet 5 inches tall and weighed approximately 125 lbs. Her estimated age was somewhere between 17-20. A set of red lips was drawn on the upper portion of her left breast with lipstick, postmortem. The body shows evidence of a violent compression of the neck, which caused bruising, and ligature marks therefore, the official cause of death is asphyxiation by strangulation. The approximate time of death was between 10:00 p.m. and 12:00 p.m. on August 24, 1982

After reading all the reports, Chief Burns went to the white board and began listing what he considered to be important facts.

1. Name: "Jane Doe"
2. Age: Between 17-20
3. Cause of Death: Asphyxiation by Strangulation
4. Body Discovered: Put in a trunk and taken to the watershed
5. Black button found in trunk not from her clothing
6. Red fibers found in trunk not from her clothing
7. Extensive dental procedures, possible a dental student
8. White substance on slacks
9. Set of lips drawn on upper part of left breast with red lipstick
10. Previous broken toe
11. Blond hair
12. Blue eyes
13. White female
14. Killed on August 24, 1982

Chief Burns stopped writing and stared intently at the white board. *Had he discovered anything new from the file review? The most obvious thing was that the victim was murdered somewhere else and the body was taken to the watershed to dispose of. The most puzzling thing was why hadn't anyone been able to identify her, even now after all these years.*

CHAPTER 28

CHIEF BURNS DECIDED to run back to HQ and get the second case file on Sunday. When he got back home, he sat down at his desk and opened the lid on the box marked August 1986. Pulling out the first report from detective Joe Donavan he began to read.

August 24, 1986: At approximately 11:23p.m. The Frederick Police Department received a phone call stating that a body had been discovered at a clothing store at the Westridge Shopping Center. Detective George Stone from FPD was assigned the case and dispatched to the crime scene.

11:35p.m. Detective Stone: I arrived at the crime scene and spoke briefly with Security Guard Sean Brooks, who had discovered the body. The Security Guard informed me that the victim's name was Stacy Rodgers. She was working in the clothing store alone and the last time he saw her was around 8:45p.m.

At approximately 10:40p.m. while making his final round for the night he noticed that the lights were still on in the store, which was unusual. Checking the front door, he discovered that it was unlocked and at that point he knew something was wrong. Pulling his gun, he entered the store to investigate. Clearing section by section he confirmed that there was no one else in the store. When he opened the door to the rear storage room, he discovered the body lying on the floor and called the police.

11:45 Detective Stone: I entered the storage room, pulled out my notebook and began to process the crime scene. I immediately noticed a set of red lips drawn on the upper part of the victim's left breast and it reminded me of a case that the MSP had worked four years ago. I called HQ on the radio and asked the dispatcher to contact Detective Joe Donavan from MSP to assist with this case.

Detective Joe Donavan: I arrived at the crime scene at approximately 12:30a.m. and signed into the murder logbook. Detective Stone explained that he had call MSP to assist with the case due to the unusual circumstances. He guided me to the rear storage room where the body was located. After inspecting the body, I confirmed to him that there were notably similarities to the case that I had worked four years ago and never solved. Detective Stone and I agree that the two cases are somehow related and that we should re-open my cold case from four years ago.

1:45a.m. Sean Brooks, the Security Guard who discovered the body was taken to FPD HQ for questioning. During his interview, he informed us that Stacy Rodgers has a boyfriend by the name is Jimmy Often, and that he was supposed to pick-her-up after work last night. We felt like some of his answers didn't add up and he seemed nervous and agitated during the interview.

We considered him a suspect, but we have no physical evidence directly linking him to the case.

August 25, 1986, 11: 00a.m: Detective Stone and I went to Jimmy Often house for an interviewed. He denied that he was supposed to pick Stacy up last night after work and explained that around three weeks ago she found out that he had cheated on her and broke up with him. He and been calling her every day apologizing trying to get her to go back with him and finally, she agreed to see him yesterday morning.

He stated, that he arrived at Stacy's house around 9:00 a.m. and they went into the living room to talked. He begged her to forgive him for cheating and offered his high school ring back. She finally agreed to give him one more chance accepting his ring and place it on a necklace she was wearing.

The information Jimmy provided during the initial interview sounded plausible, but after interviewing some of Stacy friends no one could confirm that the two had gone back together. In fact, some of her friends stated that Jimmy had beaten her up and that was the real reason they had broken up. The high school ring was found along with a broken gold necklace on the floor next to Stacy's body. After questioning Jimmy Often, we considered him a suspect even though there is no physical evidence directly linking him to the case.

The cash register drawer and receipts were found on the counter and no money had been taken, so this wasn't a robbery. There were slight signs of a struggle, but she had not been sexually assaulted. There was some bruising on the arms, wrists, and neck and the cause of death was determined to be asphyxiation by strangulation. Detective Stone and I have concluded that, Stacy Rodgers probably knew her assailant and it's plausible that either one of our two suspects could be the killer.

Chief Burns leaned back in his chair and began to ponder the two cases, *Stacy Rodgers was positively identified by her parents, but the young lady discovered in the trunk was never identified. Stacy was nineteen years old the other girl's age was estimated between 17 and 20. Both had blonde hair and blue eyes and were both approximately the same height. Stacy was an honor student in high school wrote poetry and hoped to study Business Management in college. She had a part-time job and drove a four-year-old car that she had paid for herself. A miniscule amount of DNA was discovered at the murder scene, but DNA technology was still comparatively crude back then, and cost prohibitive so no DNA samples were ever submitted for testing.*

It appeared to Chief burns that the detectives investigating the case did have some circumstantial evidence, but it wasn't enough to make an arrest.

He set down in his chair thinking, *DNA technology has advanced to where an analyst can now extract a DNA profile from material that is left by just a touch. I'll need to get the DNA samples submitted to the FBI Lab in Quantico Virginia for testing right away. After my extensive review of the two cases the most obvious question is, why four years apart. Was he in jail or are there other lipstick murders that we just don't know about?* He went to the white board and began writing.

1. Name: Stacy Rodgers
2. Age: 19
3. Cause of Death: Asphyxiation by Strangulation
4. Body Discovered In rear storage room of clothing store
5. Hair and fibers were discovered, but were the victim's
6. Security guard discovered body
7. Set of lips drawn on upper part of left breast with red lipstick
8. Blond hair
9. Blue eyes
10. 5' 5"
11. 125 lbs.
12. White Female
13. Killed August 24, 1986

CHAPTER 29

June 14, 1991

DEANO'S BAR AND GRILL located on North Market Street is one of Frederick's most popular local hangouts. The rapist wasn't crazy about going there, because it's a favorite watering hole of FPD finest.

Approaching the front door, he nodding to the big bouncer who happens to be an off-duty police officer collecting the cover charge. Entering the bar, he saw a friend across the room sitting on his favorite bar stool and waved. Passing several tables, he took his usual inconspicuous spot at a small table near the rear corner of the bar. *Everyone hides who they are at least some of the time. And sometimes you just want to forget who you are all together.*

The waitress came over to the table and asked, "the usual?"

"Yes, thanks," he said staring at her ass as she walked away.

A few minutes later the blonde waitress returned with his Michelob and sit it down on the table. "Anything else I can do for you," she asked in a flirting way.

"No, but thanks anyway," he replied.

She turned to walk away, and he couldn't help thinking, *she has a great ass, nice tits and always flirts with me, but she's not my type.*

A local rock band was setting up their equipment on the stage near the front door. He began scanning the room and his head suddenly stopped cold when he saw her. They're sitting across the room, was a beautiful young woman who looked to be about twenty-two or twenty-three years old. She had long brown hair, a nice slender body, and was wearing a short blue dress. The dress had a low-cut V-neck in front showing most of her cleavage. "Now that's my type," he whispered to himself.

His dark passenger had returned *I'm back in the belly of the beast. I feel like I've been holding my head under water holding my breath and now I can finely breath so how come it's so suffocating in here.*

A few hours later, it was near closing time and he watched closely as the girl in the blue dress staggered towards the front door. He quickly paid his tab and left the bar a few steps behind her. Standing on the front porch, he watched as she stumbled down North Market Street.

He began following her picking up his pace as she turned right on West Third Street. His heart was pounding harder as he looked ahead, trying to determine where to make his move. Suddenly, it came to him, *up ahead there's an alleyway with a tall wooden gate between two storefront buildings with a small courtyard in the rear, that's the place.*

Reaching in his coat pocket he took out a set of rubber gloves and pulled them on. He put on a mask and dragged it down over his head. He was closing-in on her fast now and was only ten steps away.

Unexpectedly, she heard someone approaching from behind and turned. The rapist punched her in the mouth, and she began falling backwards feeling a shocking pain. He grabbed her arm to keep her from falling, placed his hand over her mouth and said, "don't make a fucking sound or I'll kill you."

Shoving his gun into her ribs he began pushing her through the small alleyway in between two storefronts. Opening the tall wooden gate, they stepped inside, and he swung the gate close behind them.

Although it was late at night and a warm breeze was in the air, sweat trickled downward between her breast and along the small of her back. Her hands were clammy, and her mouth was so dry she could barely swallow. She told herself don't be afraid of dying, because living could be much worst.

"Please don't hurt me," she mumbled looking through the holes of the mask at the intense look in his eyes. He put the gun in his holster and stepped closer to her. "I like brunettes," he whispered, and both his hands were in her hair, grasping each side of her head. He kissed her, and the smell of stale cigarettes made her gag. He put his arms around her and hauls her against his body, squeezing her tightly. One hand remained in her hair, the other traveled down her spine to her waist and down to her behind. His hand flexes over her backside and squeezes hard. He holds her against his hips, and she can feel his erection.

Forcing her to the ground, he pulled up her dress and ripped off the skimpy black underwear. Pulling a condom from his pocket, he tore the end off the package with his teeth and quickly put it on. "I'm going to fuck you now," he whispered as he positions the head of his erection at the entrance of her sex and slams into her.

"You're hurting me!" She cried out as she could feel a weird pinching sensation deep inside as he ripped through her. It was so intrusive, so overwhelming.

She could feel his weight on her, holding her down he was having his way with her because she was too frightened to fight back. He pounded on picking up speed, merciless, a relentless rhythm, as tears ran down her cheeks. There were two sharp thrusts, and he freezes, pouring himself into her as he finds his release.

Pulling out of her, he stood up and removed a brown paper bag from his pocket. Pulling off the condom and the rubber gloves, he dropped them inside the Brown paper bag. Folding-up the bag, he placed it inside his pocket. Squatting down to her still lying on the ground, he whispered in her ear, "Let this be our little secret, if you tell anyone, I'll find you and kill you, got it."

"Yes," she mumbled and nodded her head.

Brushing himself off, he hurried through the wooden gate pulling off his mask and stuffing it inside his pocket. When he reached the corner of Third Street, he turned left onto North Market Street where he had parked his car and headed home.

The rapist and his wife lived in a nice neighborhood in the Montgomery Village subdivision just off East Street. Turning into his driveway, he couldn't help reflecting on what he had just done. He glanced into the rearview mirror on the windshield and saw a big smirk on his face. It was as if he was confirming to himself that he had gotten away with another rape.

Slowly, he got out of the car and walked up the driveway, stuck the key in the front door, and entered. He wasn't surprised to see his wife sitting at the dining room table waiting-up for him.

"Where in the fuck have you been? It's two thirty in the morning and I've been trying to reach you for hours."

"You know I always go out for a few drinks on Friday night with the guys," he replied.

"I know, but why in the do you always have to close up the place, you know I'm seven months pregnant and I need you to be here for me. This pregnancy has been difficult and as you know the doctor said it was dangerous for me to have a baby."

"I'm sorry, but I've got to get to bed, I am tired, and we can discuss this tomorrow."

He undressed and fell into bed hopping my morning she'd forget the whole thing.

CHAPTER 30

MEGAN WIPED AWAY the tears from her cheeks and clutched the sides of her dress pulling it down over her hips. Trying desperately to get to her feet, she began sinking helplessly back down to her knees and cried hysterically.

Petrified that the rapist could return, she knew that she had to get out of there. She was finally able struggled to her feet and wandered through the big wooden gate. Turning right she amble past a storefront and saw a big black double door and began beating on the door. "Help, someone please help me," she cried out.

After several minutes, Mrs. Dorthey the little lady who lived there came to the door and said, "who is it," without opening the door.

"I've been raped, please open the door so I can use your telephone."

Slowly, the door inched open and a small frail lady was standing there in her nightgowned with gray hair wrapped in a small bun. Megan was standing on the doorstep with dried blood on her lip, her dress was disheveled and torn in several places, she whimpered, "can I please use your telephone to call the police?"

"Yes, of course, you're safe now," Mrs. Dorthey said and grabbed her arm pulling her inside, locking the door behind them."

"Thank you," Megan replied.

"Come on, the phone is in the living room."

Megan sat down on the couch, grabbed the receiver from the end table and called the police.

"FPD, how can I help you?"

"I've been raped, please send someone right away."

The voice on the other end of the phone said, "What's your name and location?" She said, "My name is Megan Kelly and I am at 106 West Third Street."

"Is the assailant gone?"

"Yes, I'm at the house next store to where it happened."

"Ok, stay on to the phone, I'm sending the police right away."

The dispatcher tried to keep Megan calm by talking to her but found himself struggling for words. He thought, *no matter how many of these calls you take; it's still difficult to talk to someone who's been raped.*

He had been through all the training, but training doesn't really compare to the real thing

Finally, two police officers rang the doorbell and Mrs. Dorthey swung the door open, "come-in, she's here in the living room."

One of the officers was a male, Evan Howell and the other was a female, Sherry Gross. They did an initial interview with the victim and explained to Megan that they were going to take her to Frederick Memorial Hospital. "Why do I need to go the hospital, I'm not hurt, except for my busted lip," she replied trying to wipe away the dried blood.

"We need to get a rape kit test done that will include collecting evidence from your body and clothing. They'll be looking for hair and fiber from the rapist. This is important because it could lead to the capture of the man who did this. Evan, the forensics' guys are here to go over the crime scene, why don't you stay here to oversee that, and I'll take Megan to the hospital," Officer Gross suggested.

"Sounds like a plan," Officer Howell replied.

Officer Gross stood up and extended her hand to Megan helping her up from the couch. Megan thanked Mrs. Dorthey several times for answering the door. They exited the house and approach Officer Gross's cruiser sitting in the middle of Third Street with the lights flashing. Officer Gross opened the passenger door helping Megan inside the car and drove her to the hospital.

She waited in the lobby while the doctor did the examination and thirty minutes later the doctor came through the double sliding glass doors, "Officer Gross you can see Megan now. I'll have a full report for you by tomorrow, but for now, there is evidence that she was raped. However, we didn't find any semen inside her and the only hair and fiber we discovered was from her."

"Thanks Doc, I appreciate it. What 's the room number?"

"It's 302, through those double doors, down the hall and to the right," the doctor explained.

Officer Gross slowly sauntered down the hallway towards Megan's room. She entered the room and said, "I'm sorry Megan but I need to get your statement while it's fresh in your mind. Where were you heading at that time in the morning?"

"I was on my way home from Deano's and he came up behind and dragged me through the alleyway to the courtyard," she explained as tear's trickled down her cheeks.

"It's ok Megan, did any strange men approach you at the bar?"

"No, not really, I know a lot of people that hang out there. He must have followed me when I left, I should have never worn that short dress and he probably saw how drunk I was. He had a gun and I thought he was going to kill me."

"Listen Megan this is not your fault. The doctor said she didn't find any semen, was the assailant wearing a condom?"

"Yes, and he was also wearing rubber gloves."

"Did you see what he did with the condom when he was finished?"

"He pulled a brown paper bag from his coat pocket and dropped the condom and the gloves inside the bag. After that he folded-up the bag and put it back in his coat pocket."

"Did he have any tattoos, distinguishing marks or any distinguishing features?"

"Yes, I saw a small tattoo that looked like a cross on his left wrist."

After several more questions, Officer Gross said, "Come-on, let me give you a ride home."

Megan gave Officer Gross directions to her apartment, which was on West Third Street, one block from where she was attacked. She accompanied her inside the apartment, to ask her a few more questions, but most of all she wanted to try to comfort her and make her feel secure. "Megan, do you think you can come to HQ in the next day or two."

"What for, I already gave you my statement."

"I'll need you to sign the statement once I get it all typed up and I'd like to get a composite drawing of the assailant and his tattoo. Also, I know it's a long shot, but I'd like for you to look through our weapons books and try to identify the type of weapon the assailant had?"

"I'll try, but I'm not sure if I can."

"Ok," Officer Gross replied thinking, *that's going to have to do for now, I don't want to push her any harder, I know she's gone through a terrible life changing experience and besides I'm turning the case over to the Detectives tomorrow anyway.*

CHAPTER 31

CHIEF BURNS WENT TO BED around 10:00 p.m. and was awaken at approximately 3:00 a. m. when his phone began to ring. Still half asleep, he grabbed the receiver from the nightstand, "Chief Burns."

"Chief, this is the dispatcher, I'm sorry to bug you at this time in the morning but there's been another rape and I thought you would want to know right away."

"Who's took the call?"

"Officer's Sherry Gross and Evan Howell took the initial call and will be handing the file over to the detectives in the morning, I'll give them a call first thing?"

"That won't be necessary, their busy working with me on the lipstick murder cases. I'm going to assign Officer Faye-Lynn Johnson to the rape cases. Call her in the morning and asked her to report to my office at 8:00 a.m."

Chief Burns reached over and turned off the lamp on the nightstand hopeful that he'd be able to get back to sleep. Unfortunately, that didn't happen, he tossed and turned the rest of the night eventually climbing out of bed at 6:00 a.m.

After taking a quick shower, he got dressed and headed off to McDonald's for some coffee on the way to HQ. He was trying to hurry because he wanted time to take one last look at Officer's Faye-Lynn Johnson's personnel file before she arrived.

He sat down at his desk, opened the top drawer and pulled out her personnel file. Looking over it very carefully, he noticed that she had won many awards and citations. On paper she was impressive, *I believed she'd make a great detective*, he concluded just before she arrived.

At 8:00 a.m. sharp, Officer Johnson knocked on the office door and entered, "You wanted to see me Chief?"

"Please have a seat Officer Johnson there's something I'd like to discuss with you. You may have heard, that there was another rape last night. That's the third one now in the last nine months and it's unacceptable for this to be happening in our city. I'm going to reassign you away from your patrolmen duties to work these cases and I'll need you to recommend a squad leader as your replacement."

"Are you sure about this Chief, isn't detective Wayne working the rape cases."

"The detectives are working on the Lipstick Murders and I think a woman should be the lead on the rape cases anyway. In my experience the victims are always reluctant to open-up to a male officer."

Officer Johnson pause before speaking, "I'm not sure I can handle it Chief, I wouldn't want to let these women down."

"Officer Johnson, you told me you wanted to be a detective and you need to start somewhere. Although I don't have it in the budget right now for a third detective, this case will be a great on-the-job training experience for you. I have a lot of confidence in your abilities and I know you can do this."

"Will I report to detective Wayne since he is officially assigned the other two rape cases?"

"No, you'll be handling all three cases, I spoke to Officer Gross who took statements from all three victims and I believe the cases are related. Detective Wayne will provide you the other case files and you'll be reporting directly to me. In the meantime, get the case file from Officer Gross from last night. Once you've had a chance to review all the files we can talk again and map out a strategy."

It was nine o'clock Monday morning when the detectives showed up at Chief Burns office for their scheduled meeting. "Good morning Detectives, I don't know if you've heard yet, but there was another rape Friday night, down on West Third Street and I've decided to assign the rape cases to Officer Johnson."

"Why are you assigning her my cases Chief, she's not a detective," Detective Wayne asked with a sharp tone.

"She passed the detective's exam a while back and these cases will be good on-the-job training for her. Besides, I need you guys to give your full attention to the lipstick murder cases. Please turn over your case files to Officer Johnson and fill her in on what you have so far Detective Wayne," Chief Burns replied.

"Yes sir."

"Do you have any new information on the first unsolved murder case that we discussed last week," Chief Burns asked.

"I interviewed the Medical Examiner and he confirmed that the victim's dental work may have been done at a dental school. In other words, the work wasn't good enough to have been done by a real dentist. When the body was discovered, the dental records were only sent to schools in Maryland.

After confirming this information, I sent the x-rays to dental schools in Virginia, West Virginia and Pennsylvania and among the three states there are thirty-one schools. I asked them to compare the records of all the students they have on file from around the time the body was discovered. I know it's a long shot but hopefully once we get the list, we can exclude some of them based on age and so forth. I'm waiting to hear back from the schools, but this is going to take a while," Detective Thomas detailed.

"Thanks, detective. Anything new on the button and clothing fibers Detective Wayne?"

"I contacted the FBI agent who worked the case and a forensic expert for interviews. I've met with both and neither one of them had much more to offer other than what's in the case files. The forensics' expert did say that their lab had confirmed that the red fibers were from a sweater type material. He also stated that there was a small amount of black thread in the button holes of the large button found in the trunk and it had minute traces of the same red fibers as the other fibers found." Detective Wayne explained.

"What does this tell us?" Chief Burns asked.

"The black button and the red fibers found in the trunk came from the same item and none of this evidence is consistent with anything the victim was wearing. Therefore, the FBI's believes that the murderer could have been wearing a red sweater with black buttons during the disposal of the body."

"This is a good start guys, detective Wayne I'd like you to interview the FBI agent who handled the Stacy Rodgers murder case. Detective Thomas you can talk to the Medical Examiner and see if you can get any new leads. I understand in her case there were two suspects, but an arrest was never made, we need to figure out why."

CHAPTER 32

I SAT DOWN AT MY DESK to catch up on some paperwork after my great meeting with Chief Burns. I was anxious to clean up a couple of old case files, so I could devote all my time to the rape cases. Also, I had to figure out whom to recommend as my replacement for squad leader.

I leaned back in my chair and cracked a big smile thinking, *finally the big break I've been longing for. I'm not a hundred percent sure where to start on the biggest assignment of my career, but I guess I figure it out.*

I saw the detectives coming out of Chief Burns office and yelled, "hey Duke, did the Chief tell you to provide me the rape case files? He wants me start reviewing them right away," I explained.

"The files aren't here Faye-Lynn, I took them home to study. I'll bring them in for you tomorrow."

"Thanks Duke I appreciate it."

"Sure, no problem," he replied turning to walk away.

Officer Gross was a little surprise when Megan Kelly called because she had barely left her apartment in the last three weeks. She said she wanted to do the right thing and didn't want this to happen to anyone else.

Pulling to the curb on West Third Street, Officer Gross looked over and saw Megan coming out of her apartment building. She opened the passenger door and climbed in.

"Thanks for giving me a ride Officer Gross, I really appreciate it."

"No problem, thanks for coming to HQ, I know this is difficult for you. By the way Officer Faye-Lynn Johnson will be handling your case. She's a great police officer and very smart."

Megan just nodded as they drove off towards HQ.

Officer Gross pulled into the driveway leading to the rear parking lot at HQ. They exited the car and walked down the sidewalk to the front of the building. Starting up the steps, they passed detectives Wayne and Thomas leaving the building.

"Good morning ladies," detective Wayne said as they passed.

A frightened look came over Megan's face as she thought she recognize a voice. But she quickly dismissed it she had heard that same voice in her head a million times the last three weeks, it just wouldn't go away.

I came out to meet Megan and took her back to my cubicle where I had several large books with pictures of handguns. I explained to Megan that I wanted her to look through the books and identify the gun that the man had threatened her with.

"Do you think you can do that?" I asked.

"Yes, I think so, I'll never forget what the gun looked like, he was waving it in my face and sliding it down between my breasts intimidating me. And then he would laugh when he saw the fear in my eyes."

Megan began looking at pictures of guns and eliminating them one by one, finally after thirty-five minuets, she said, "this is it."

"Are you absolutely sure," I asked.

"I am sure, there is no doubt in my mind," Megan replied.

Megan had identified a 38 police special as the weapon the rapist had threatened her with, and I was a little surprised to say the least. I had to ask myself, *what does this mean?*

"Megan, I'm going to bring our sketch artist over and I want you to work with him, so we can get a composite drawing of the rapist. We also need you to describe the tattoo you saw on the assailant's wrist, so we can get a drawing of that," I explained.

Megan described every detail she could remember to the sketch artist about the rapist and when they were finished, I thanked her for coming in. After she left, I sat at my desk typing up a report to describe today's activities. I opened the folder to insert my report and glanced down at the composite drawings, *the drawing of the face doesn't help much, he had on a mask and the drawing really could be anyone.*

I looked down at the drawing of the tattoo and snatched it up to get a closer look. *I've seen this tattoo before or at least one like it, I need to get the other case files from detective Wayne to see if there's any mention of a tattoo. Also, I need to interview the other two rape victims as soon as possible.*

CHAPTER 33

CHIEF BURNS BEGAN REVEWING the third unsolved murder case file but there were just too many distractions. He finally left work for the day and decided to take the file home to review over the weekend.

After dinner, he grabbed the box marked August 1990 and headed upstairs to his office. Sitting down at his desk, he opened the lid pulling out the first report from detective Dominick Thomas and began to read.

August 25, 1990: At approximately 4:07 p.m. the Frederick Police Department received a phone call stating that a body had been discovered along a dirt road just off West South Street. Detective's Duke Wayne and Dominick Thomas from FPD were assigned the case and dispatched to the crime scene.

4:27 p.m. Detective Wayne and I arrived at the crime scene and signed into the murder logbook. I spoke briefly with the Officer in charge Faye-Lynn Johnson. She informed me that two homeless men were walking up the road looking for cans to sell when they happened upon a pile of trash. They began digging through the trash and noticed that there were two feet protruding out from the bottom of a rolled-up carpet.

4:45 p.m. Detective Wayne and I unrolled the carpet and discovered the body of a young white female, Tracy Roberts. She was seventeen years of age, blond hair, blue eyes, and approximately five feet four inches tall. The victim's purse was discovered next to the body. Tracy was last seen by her parents at approximately 1:30 p.m. that afternoon.

5:23 p.m. the coroner arrived and began examining the body pointing out a set of red lips drawn on the upper part of the victim's left breast with lipstick. She noted that there were no visible track marks, but there's was a foreign substance under the victim's fingernails. There's no evidence of sexual assault; therefore, the victim could have known her assailant. The coroner stated that the victim had only been dead for a few hours and the preliminary examination appears to show the cause of death to be asphyxiation by strangulation.

As Chief Burns was reading the case file, he felt tears welling up in his eyes for the third time in a week, *you're not supposed to make murder cases personal, but that's hard to avoid when you have a daughter nearly the same age as the three girls who were murdered.*

5:45 Officer Faye-Lynn Johnson approached the body and saw the red lips drawn on the victim's chest and explained to the detectives that this murder could be the work of a serial killer.

We instructed Officer Johnson to take the two homeless men to HQ for questioning.

6:20 Detective Wayne and I arrived at HQ and began questioning the two homeless men who had discovered the body. After the interview, we were able to rule them out as suspects placing a lot of weight on the fact that they had immediately contacted police after discovering the body.

During the interview we were informed that other homeless people were living in the woods near the crime scene and we asked Officer Johnson too to bring them in for questioning. There was a total of seven, including the two we had already interviewed, six men and one woman. We interviewed the woman and quickly ruled her out.

We then interviewed the other men and there was only one who stood out. Ronald Evans, who was a mentally ill black man. He stood over 6 feet tall and weighed around 220 Lbs. Recently, Ronald had been released from prison after serving three years of a ten-year sentence. He had a lengthy rap sheet, which included multiple sex offenses, and according to his file, he had been diagnosed with severe mental illnesses, including a diagnosis of pedophilia and paranoid schizophrenia.

Ronald Evans became a suspect, but we didn't have enough to hold him and had to released him after twenty-four. We set up surveillance and followed the suspect for several weeks without turning up any new evidence or leads. Senior management decided it was too expensive to continue the surveillance and ordered it to be discontinued due to budget constraints.

December 18, 1990: An eleven-year-old girl's body was discovered who'd been sexually assaulted and killed with a baseball bat. Ronald Evans became the prime suspect when the young girl was seen with him on surveillance cameras in a small grocery store two blocks from where the body was discovered. He was charged with first-degree murder and first-degree sexual assault and was in prison awaiting trial.

After our extensive investigation into Ronald Evans background, we concluded that he had nothing to do with the murder of Tracy Roberts. He was considered a suspect at first, but she wasn't sexually assaulted so that didn't fit Ronald Evans MO and he had an alibi for the day Tracy was killed.

December 30,1990 Ronald Evans was beaten to death in Prison at the age of fifty-three.

Chief Burns jumped up from his chair and started writing down important items on the white board.

1. Name: Tracy Roberts

2. Age: 17
3. Strangled
4. Rolled up in a carpet
5. No hair or fibers found on the body
6. 2 homeless men discovered body
7. Red lipstick set of lips drawn on left breast
8. 5' 4"
9. 128 lbs.
10. Body found in wooded area

Setting back in his chair, he began to think about the case, *the Detectives probably screw up on this case by locking in on Ronald Evans so quick. He was a bad guy all right, but he just wasn't the one who killed Tracy Roberts, but if he didn't do it, who did and was it the same person who killed the other two girls?*

CHAPTER 34

BARBARA'S HUSBAND LEFT work early to drive her to a doctor's appointment. He had been concerned lately about her being sick all the time with the pregnancy. They entered the doctor's office and approached the receptionist desk, "Hi, I have an appointment with Doctor Moore for two o'clock," Barbara stated.

"Please have a seat, we'll be with you shortly," the receptionist replied.

A nurse exited through a side door calling out Barbara's name and directed her to examination room number one. After taking her blood pressure, she handed Barbara a paper gown and asked her to get undressed. A few minutes later Dr. Moore entered and gave her a thorough examination, "Please get dressed Barbara, I'll speak to you and your husband in a few minutes."

Five minutes later Dr. Moore approached them in the waiting area, "I wanted to let you know that your examination went very well, however, as a precaution I'd like to get you admitted to Frederick Memorial hospital."

"Is there something you're not telling us Dr. Moore?" Barbara's husband asked.

"As you know Barbara's had two miscarriages and she is over eight months pregnant. We're at a very critical stage and I want to ensure that she doesn't have any complications during these last few weeks. If she's in the hospital we can keep a close eye on her," Dr. Moore explained.

"It's not a problem Doctor, you discuss this with us early on, but I'll need to run home to get a few things," Barbara replied.

"No problem, why don't we meet at the hospital at 3:30 so I can get you admitted," Doctor Moore responded.

"Ok, we'll see you there," Barbara's husband replied.

Barbara began lecturing her husband during the drive home, telling him not to be hanging out with the guys drinking every night while she was in the hospital. He nodding his head agreeing with her and telling her what she wanted to hear, all the while thinking, *women can be so fucking stupid, they believe almost anything you tell them, of course I am going to go out, I might even get laid.*

Barbara gathered up the bag she had previously packed and a few other odds and ends.

They left their house and stopped at McDonalds to get a bite to eat before they drove off towards the hospital.

Driving down the road her husband began reflecting to the first time he had rape someone. He was in college, met a girl at a bar and put a date rape drug into her drink. The drugs were easy to get in college and just as easy to slip into someone's drink. He practically had to carry the girl to his car before he raped her. Driving about four miles from the bar, he left her along the side of the road. He worried for months that she would remember what he had done, but as time went on, he knew that he had gotten away with it. After that he did it several more times, each time getting a little bolder and taking more chances.

One day he met Barbara and their relationship was completely different. They had several classes together and became good friends, lovers, and then soul mates. It was the first real relationship that he had ever experience. They dated for two years while in college, then he asked her to marry him and she accepted. He had hoped that after falling in love and marring Barbara that his dark passenger would disappear. After all, she was a beautiful woman and he could have her anytime he wanted her. The urges did go away for a while, but it didn't seem to be something that he could control.

They arrived at the hospital a little after three and the person at the front desk asked them to have a seat and wait for the doctor. She arrived a few minutes later, and got Barbara admitted. Her husband told her that he had to take care of a few things and he would be back around six during visiting hours.

Arriving at the hospital at 6:30, he went to his wife's room, approached the bed kissing her a quick touch of the lips and asked, "How you are feeling."

She began to rattle on about how bad she felt, and he quickly zoned out thinking, *I've been listening to this dam whining and complaining for months now, I'll be glad when it's over.* He always wanted a child, but he could barely stand to look at Barbara being pregnant, in fact it turned his stomach. She was beautiful when they'd met with a stunning body and long gorgeous brown hair. But she had cut her hair, gained way too much weight and her breasts were like watermelons. When he looked at her, his only thought was, *she'll never be as young and beautiful as she once was.*

CHAPTER 35

I SCHEDULED A MEETING with Chief Burns to discuss the rape cases he had assigned me. I knocked on his door promptly at 9:00 a.m. and entered his office. "Morning Chief."

"Good morning Officer Johnson, please have a seat."

"Thank you, Sir."

"Did you get a chance to review the files in the three rape cases?"

"I've gone over Megan Kelly's statement several times and there's not a lot to go on, but I do have a couple of things that I'm pursuing. The victim said on the night of the rape that the assailant was brandishing a weapon. I had her come down to HQ to go through our current weapons books and she made a positive identification on thirty-eight police special."

"She was certain about that?" the Chief asked.

"Yes, I checked and double checked with her to make sure she wasn't guessing. She seems to know a lot about guns in fact her father was a collector. After she left, I began writing my report for the case file and suddenly realized the weapon she had identified is FPD's standard issue."

"Yes, that's true Officer Johnson, but keep in mind a thirty-eight can also be purchased by anyone on the street with a little cash."

"Yes sir."

"Any other leads?" the Chief asked.

"Megan described a tattoo of a small cross on the assailant left wrist to our sketch artist. The weird thing is that I think I've seen that tattoo somewhere before, I just haven't figured out where."

"What, are you sure?"

"I think so, but I'm not certain."

"Did you find any connections to the other two rape cases?"

"Detective Wayne hasn't provided me with those files yet, he said he took them home to study and he keeps forgetting to bring them in."

"Ok, I'll speak with him again, you need those files, I believe all three cases are related and I want to catch this bastard before he rapes again. That's all for now Officer Johnson, thanks for the update."

I exited the Chief's Office and headed back to my desk hoping that I hadn't gotten Duke in trouble.
He was my friend and I wasn't trying to throw him under the bus.

Chief Burns was pissed off that Detective Wayne hadn't turned over the case files to Officer Johnson. He picked up his phone and dialed his extension. He waited to the fifth ring to answer the phone which pissed-off the Chief even more. No one had seen the new Chief pissed off, it doesn't happen to often, but Officer Wayne was testing his patience and he didn't like it.

Finally, he picked up the phone and said, "Detective Wayne, can I help you?"

"Detective Wayne, I asked you last Monday to provide the two rape case files to Officer Johnson. She tells me that you still haven't turned them over which is impeding her investigation. You get those fucking case files on her desk by close of business today or I'll write your ass up, do you understand?"

"Yes Sir," he replied hanging up the phone with a strange look on his face. Looking across the desk towards his partner, he said to Detective Thomas, "I wander who stuck a crawl up his ass?"

Detective Thomas just laughed his big burley laugh and said, "what's up."

"I guess he's pissed because I haven't given the files for the rape cases to Faye-Lynn yet. I just forgot them this morning, I don't know what the fucking big deal is?" Detective Wayne said glancing towards Faye-Lynn with a strange look on his face.

Chief Burns leaned back in his chair thinking about what Officer Johnson had told him, *she may be on to something, but I don't want her to jump to any conclusions just yet.*

CHAPTER 36

I FINALLY RECEIVED the two case files from Detective Wayne and read through them several times. I was looking for something, anything that might help me solve my first big case. But just like the first case, there was no physical evidence. I began to wonder if Detective Wayne had done a follow-up interview with either of the victim's, there's is no mention of it in the case files.

I set-up appointments with the two women and spent several hours interviewing them. They told me they had given a statement to the female police officer on the night of the rapes but hadn't spoken with anyone from FPD since.

Both victims provided almost identical description of the person who had raped them. This was the same person who raped Megan Kelly, I was sure of it. I couldn't help but think, *this information is critical to solving these cases and would have been totally missed if I hadn't done the follow-up interviews.* I was dumbfounded that Detective Wayne hadn't done it, because it's standard protocol. This isn't like him, he's a good detective and a close friend, *and I just don't get it.*

I received a call at three a.m. from FPDs dispatcher, "Hello Officer Johnson, sorry to wake you but Chief Burns wants you to go to the Rocky Ridge Subdivision to see the resident at 19 West Carroll Street, for an attempted robbery."

"I'm not working robbery right now, the Chief assigned me to the rape cases." I explained.

"I know, but we don't think it was really an attempted robbery. We think it could be related to your investigation judging from the incident described by the victim. If you decide that isn't the case, you can turn the file over to the robbery squad tomorrow morning."

"Ok, no problem, I'll get over there as soon as possible."

Hanging up the phone I quickly got dressed in my tee shirt and jeans. I hurried out the front door and it was nearly 3:30 by the time I arrived at the address provided by the dispatcher. The house was located on a cul-de-sac with three other houses. I climbed out of my police cruiser and approached the front porch. I knocked on the door and after a few minutes a voice from inside yell, "Who is it?"

"Frederick Police Department," I responded.

The door finally opened and standing before me was a very nice-looking young lady with long brown hair and a slender build.

It was as if I was seeing the same two women that I'd interviewed yesterday *the rapist has a type.*

"Hi, I'm Officer Faye-Lynn Johnson, I understand you reported an attempted robbery?"

"Yes, please come-in and have a seat."

I entered the house, sat down on the couch opposite the young lady in the recliner and asked, "Can you give me your full name for my report."

"I'm Donna Jenkins and someone tried to rob me right out there in my own parking lot, can you believe it?"

"Can you give me a description of the assailant?" I asked.

"It happened pretty fast, but I think he was about 5' 6" or 5' 7" and maybe weighed around 180 pounds. He had on a mask and white rubber gloves."

"Please tell me what happened?"

"I parked my car and walked around to the passenger side to get a few things. I grabbed my stuff off the front seat, turned and there he was, coming towards me. He was about twenty feet from me, and I was scared to death. I didn't know what to do, and then I started pressing my car alarm on my key ring. The horn started blaring and he stopped in his tracks, spun around, ran towards his car and took off."

"Was there anything that you recognized about him, I mean why do you think he picked you?" I asked.

"I'm not sure, my band played at a club tonight and I thought someone was following me when I pulled out of the parking lot. But when I got on the highway, there was a lot of other cars behind me, so I shrug it off, figuring it was probably my imagination"

"Did you happen to get a tag number, even a partial could help."

"Yes, as he started to pull out, I ran towards his car, I know it was a stupid thing to do, but I made up my mind that I had to get his tag number. As soon as I got inside the house, I wrote it down, so I wouldn't forget."

Donna got up from the recliner and handed me a piece of paper with two words written on it, "Local GOV."

After reading it, I asked, "Are you certain that's what was on the tag?"

"I am sure," she replied.

I left Donna's house, climbed inside my car and turned on the dash lights to do a quick review of my notes. After skimming through them for the second time, I've come to some conclusions, *Donna's dam lucky that she was able to scare off the assailant otherwise she could have been the next rape victim. I believe the same person committed all three rapes, but the most troubling information is that the assailant carries 38 police special and drives a car with a local government tag, just like mine.*

CHAPTER 37

September 5, 1991

BARBARA'S HUSBAND WAS visiting the hospital every night to spend a few hours with her. Her room was nice, but expensive with a single bed. There were a couple of monitors on one end with a TV mounted to the wall on the other end. It had its own bathroom and two chairs off to the side of the bed.

He felt obligated to visit her but found himself watching the clock half talking and half listing, thinking the entire time, *I can't wait to get the fuck out of here.* Barbara seemed very weak tonight and was sicker than he had ever seen her before. Her doctor had warned that this was going to be a difficult pregnancy and could be dangerous to her health.

Dr. Sara Moore was an incredibility good doctor and had a great reputation. She checks on Barbara twice a day, once in the afternoon and again around seven at night. He glanced at the clock for the third time wondering when she was going to get there. Finally, at five after seven she entered Barbara's room and said, "How are we doing guys?"

"She seems really weak tonight Doc and she's a little sick on the stomach." Barbara's husband replied.

Dr. Moore approached the bed, leaning over to checked Barbara's blood pressure and pulse. Although Barbara's husband had known Dr. Moore for a while, he was suddenly immersed with her beauty. For the first time, he noticed how incredibly sexy she was. She had long brown hair that seemed to shimmer from the overhead lighting. Her body was sculptured with a great ass and her breasts were shaped just perfectly. Looking towards him, she smiled, and he wondered, *why he'd never noticed how attractive she was, I guess I figured, she's Barbra's doctor, so she's off limits. This was one of those moments when he wished he was like everyone else, I spend my life trying to pretend I'm not a monster, but my dark passenger is always letting me know it's still there, still alive.*

"I'll be leaving the hospital in about an hour, but I'm on call if you have any problems tonight," Dr. Moore explained.

Five minutes later Barbara's husband stood up and kissed her goodbye, "I'd better get going, visiting hours are about over anyway," he explained.

He left Barbara's room and sat in the parking lot for a half hour waiting for Dr. Moore to exit the hospital. Finally, he saw her coming through the sliding glass doors and scooted down in the seat watching her as she crossed the parking lot. She approaches a green Jeep, climbed in and pulled out of the parking lot heading North on Route 15.

He stayed at a safe distance behind her, so she wouldn't notice that he was following her. She had gone three or four miles out of town and veered off to the right on Old Frederick Road. After driving for a couple more miles she turned right onto a small dirt road. Slowing down, he drove past the road looking for a place to pull off. He found a small clearing about a quarter mile from where Dr. Moore had turned off and backed into it.

Jumping out of the car, he locked it and walked through the woods to the dirt road. He followed along the dirt road a quarter mile or so and came upon a secluded run-down old farmhouse. Standing near a big oak tree, he watched the house to see if anyone else was around. Barbara had told him, that Dr. Moore had gotten a divorce about two years ago and didn't have any children. The good doctor had explained to Barbara that being a doctor made it difficult to have any kind of lasting relationship. So, he was sure that there was no significant other, which means she's all alone tonight.

A light suddenly came on in the kitchen and the he watched carefully as the shadow of one person continued to move around. After about ten minutes, the kitchen light went out and a few minutes later an upstairs light came on. The curtains were pulled and all he could see was her silhouette, undressing in front of the window.

A few minutes later, the light went off in the bedroom and a light came on in another room. He guessed maybe it was the bathroom and thought, *she must be taking a shower, and this is a good opportunity to get closer to the house.* The house had a long wooden front porch going from end to end with two steps leading up to it. On the left side of the front door there was two old rocking chairs and on the right side was a porch swing.

He ran across the open area of the front yard and gingerly stepped up on the front porch trying not to make a sound. Suddenly, he felt a sense of relief, knowing that he had made it this far without getting discovered.

Taking a quick glance inside the window behind the rocking chairs, he didn't see anyone. He tiptoed to the other side of the front porch, and looked inside the window behind the swing, still nothing. *I need to come up with a plan to get inside the house maybe I should get the fuck out of here and pretend this never happened.*

He heard someone in the living room and looked inside the window. Dr. Moore walked across the room and suddenly it was if she was a model walking the runway just for him. She was wearing a thin nightgown that barely covered her crotch. The material was silk, and he could see her hard nipples protruding through the nightgown.

She sat down on the leather couch folding her feet underneath and turned on the television. He glanced down at the big bulge in his pants and knew at that moment, *it was too late, there's no turning back, and I've got to have her. For such a neat monster, I'm making an awfully deep mess maybe this is how evil works.*

CHAPTER 38

DR. MOORE'S PHONE RANG, "hello, yes, this is Dr. Moore."

There was a short pause while she listened to the person on the other end of the phone. "Yes, I'll be there in twenty minutes," she responded.

The rapist glanced at his watch, *who in the fuck would be calling her at this time of night?*

She stood up from the couch and he realized he had to act fast. Digging into his pocket, he pulled out a mask and a pair of rubber gloves. He pulled the mask down over his head and put on the left rubber glove. Grabbing the swing with his right hand, he slammed it in to the side of the house making a loud bang. He quickly pulled on the other glove and waited for Dr. Moore to come out to investigate.

Backing up close to the wall, he could hear the lock began to turn on the front door. She stepped out on the porch and he swung around punching her in the face. She fell backwards onto the living room floor and before she realized what was happening, he was on top of her, pressing her to the floor. He pulled a gun from his holster warning her not to make a sound and place it on the coffee table.

Suddenly, his mouth was on hers, claiming her hungrily, one hand behind her on her behind pressing her to his groin and the other one in her hair, twisting hard. He grinds his body into her, imprisoning her, his breathing ragged. The nauseating smell of stale cigarettes was sickening, as she tried to fight him off.

"Why, why do you try to defy me?" he mumbles and punches her again. Yanking down the top of her nightgown, his mouth moves to her breasts and he takes one of her nipples between his lips and tugs hard. She cries out in pain and he mistakes it for pleasure whispering, "Yes, baby, you like that don't you."

He hovers over her, staring intently into her eyes and takes a foil packet from his pocket. Ripping it open, he quickly rolls the condom on. Guiding himself into her, he closes his eyes and flexes his hips, stretching her, his mouth forming a perfect O as he exhales.

"You feel so good, I know you like it too," he murmurs.

Tears trickled down her face as she fixates on a painting hanging on the wall. "That's right, baby, feel me," he says, his voice strained. Up and down...again and again...Oh yes...Oh, baby," he groans as he finds his release, holding her still and letting go inside her.

Standing up, he took off the condom and the rubber gloves dropping them inside a brown paper bag that he had taken out of his pocket. The telephone on the coffee table began to ring and Dr. Moore lying on the floor reach for it. The rapist grabbed the phone and threw it on the floor, smashing it with his foot.

Suddenly, he was sitting on her stomach punching her again and again. She couldn't move and seemed to be fading in and out. He leaned close to her and said, "Let this be our little secret or the next time I'll kill you."

He stood up, brushing himself off, turned and hurried out the front door. Pulling off the mask, he jumped over the porch steps and began jogging down the dirt road. Turning right, he darted into the woods, heading back to the where he had left his car. He reached the car, unlocked it, jumped in and took off towards Frederick.

Sweat was running down his forehead and he began thinking, *what the hell did I just do? I've never beaten a woman that bad before, what's happening to me, my dark passenger is controlling me. I just fucked my wife's doctor. What if she recognized me?*

He turned into the driveway, but before getting out of the car he glanced up into the rearview mirror looking for that usual smirk to confirm his sense of accomplishment, but it wasn't there. This time was different he had a sick feeling about what he had done.

He walked inside the front door, grabbed a fifth of Jack Daniels off the kitchen counter top and took a big swig. He pulled a beer from the refrigerator to chase the Jack Daniels and guzzled it down. Entering the bathroom, he opened the medicine cabinet taking out a bottle of Barbara's pain pills. He dumped a handful into his palm and shoved them in his mouth.

Rambling back into the kitchen, he grabbed what was left of the Jack Daniels and beer carrying them into the bedroom. Sliding onto the edge of the bed, he reached over to the nightstand and turned on the radio. Undressing, he finished off the fifth in a couple of swigs, and then threw the bottle across the room. Lying back on the pillow, it was if he was dreaming but still awake, *actions have consequences, sooner or later, I'm going to have to pay for my dark passenger.*

CHAPTER 39

CHIEF BURNS WAS LOOKING FORWARD to meeting with the detectives to discuss the progress on the Lipstick Murder cases. Detective Thomas showed up at 8:00 a.m., their usually meeting time.

Chief Burns asked, "where in the hell is Detective Wayne, I don't appreciate it when we need to hold up a meeting because he can't make it to work on time."

"I'm sorry Chief, I've been trying to reach him all morning, but I can't get him to answer his phone or the radio," Detective Thomas explained.

"I'll deal with him later. Do you guys have anything new on the lipstick murder cases?" Chief Burns asked.

"We got word back from the FBI that the lipstick was from a different tube for each girl. The ingredients were slightly different; but they were all red, which I know, really doesn't tell us much."

"Yes, I believe all that was in the original reports. Have you found out any new information on the first victim that was found in the trunk and never identified?"

"As you know Chief, we resent the dental records out to the four states in the area. We've asked them to check against their dental student's records. We've received confirmation that we have no matches in Maryland, Virginia and West Virginia. We're still waiting for the final report from Pennsylvania."

"Detective Thomas, we really need to catch a break on the identity of the first victim, I believe she is the key to solving these murders."

"Detective Wayne is working with the FBI lab to try and find out more about the red fibers. We may have a lead on the trunk, it turns out that it was mass-produced by a manufacturer in Littlestown, Pennsylvania. They are sending us a list of stores in the area that sold the trunks. The problem is they are out of business now and all their records are in storage. They are trying to locate the information I asked for and they are supposed to get back to me by the end of the week."

"Anything else?" the Chief asked.

"We tried to interview the homeless men who discovered the body of Tracy Roberts. One of them had passed away, but the other one seems to have gotten his life together and is no longer homeless.

I interview him, and he said he couldn't remember much because it was so long ago, and he was drinking a lot in those days.

"Was there anything new?" Chief Burns asked.

"Well, he repeated pretty much the same story that's in the reports. The two men were out looking for cans to sell that morning to buy some booze and discovered the body. He said, when he first looked over and saw the feet, he had to do a double take because he thought he was hallucinating. They couldn't believe they had discovered a beautiful young girl and she was dead. He stayed with the body while his friend walked back to the Southern Market to call the police."

"So, it sounds like you didn't get anything new from him?" Chief Burns asked.

"There is one thing Chief, I asked him to think hard, if there was anything else that he could remember about that day. He explained, that there was something that came back to him later after he quit drinking. About a mile back from where they had discovered the body a vehicle had passed them driving really slow on the dirt road."

"What kind of vehicle," Chief Burns asked.

"He didn't know the make or model of the vehicle? He said all he could remember was that it was a white van, but he didn't know the year."

"I think this could be our first break in the case Detective Thomas," Chief Burns stated.

"What you mean Chief," Detective Thomas asked.

"Well it could be nothing and I may be getting ahead of myself, but I think we need to go back and check the reports in the other two cases to see if a white van was mention anywhere."

"Ok Chief, I'll get right on it."

"And find out what the hell's going on with Detective Wayne, I want to know why he's not here."

"I'll check it out Chief."

"Ok, that's all for now, thanks Detective."

CHAPTER 40

DETECTIVE WAYNE ROLLED OVER, rubbing his eyes and glanced up at the alarm clock. "Holy fuck," *I'm three hours late for my morning meeting and I'm already on the Chief's shit list. I'll need a dam good excuse for this one, I've got to get a quick shower and go to the office.*

After his shower, Detective Wayne got dressed as fast as he could and was about to head out the door when he noticed the phone recorder blinking. He pressed the message button and saw that he had, twenty-three messages. He began to listen to them and realized that the last few were from his partner. They had started around 7:00 a.m. this morning and were something to the effect of, "Where in the fuck are you?"

He rewound the tape all the way back to the beginning and listen to the first message. It was from the hospital around 10:30 last night, "Mr. Wayne, can you please come to the hospital as soon as possible, your wife has developed some serious complications and we need your permission to operate?"

He ran out of the house, jumped into his car and drove as fast as he could to the hospital. When he got there, he parked in front of the sliding glass doors, sprang out of his police cruiser and hurried inside. He jogged past the candy stripers at the information desk, down the hall and turned right into his wife's room. A nurse was standing near Barbara's empty bed, which was freshly made.

"Where's my wife? Is she in the operating room having the baby? What's going on?"

A doctor approached him and asked, "Are you Barbara Wayne's husband?"

"Yes, I'm Duke Wayne, can you please tell me what the hell is going on."

"Mr. Wayne, we tried to reach you several times last night when your wife developed serious complications with her pregnancy. We also contacted her doctor and she informed us that she was on the way to the hospital, but never arrived. The Emergency Room doctors did their best but were unable to save your wife or the baby. I'm sorry to inform you that they were pronounced dead at eleven twenty-seven last night, I'm truly sorry for your loss."

Detective Wayne, couldn't speak, he simply turned around in a daze and walked down the long hallway.

Exiting through the sliding glass doors, he slowly climbed into his police cruiser. As he drove away, he began thinking *I can never forgive myself for what I've done. I was raping my wife's doctor at the exact time she was dying on the operating table.*

Pulling into his driveway, he exited the car and slowly walked up the sidewalk to the front door unlocking it. Stepping inside the house he locked the door and walked over to the refrigerator pulling out a six-pack of beer. Going into the living room, he set the beer down on the coffee table and entered the bathroom. Opening the Medicine cabinet, he grabbed four vials of pills not bothering to read the labels.

Going back to the living room, he sat down on the couch and opened the first beer and one of the vials of pills. He thrust a hand full of pills inside his mouth and washes them down with a beer. He gagged a few times, but eventually managed to swallow all of them. He opened another beer and another vial and started the process all over again.

Removing his 38 police special from his shoulder holster, he looked at the barrel to make sure it was full of bullets and laid the gun down on the coffee table next to the vials of pills.

Dropping his head back on the couch, he closes his eyes and his mind began to wonder, *yesterday, I was hopeful of a new me, a new life, and a new baby. But now I'm trapped in the clutches of a memory. I've spent my life pretending I'm not a monster and I've lived in darkness a long time. I'm drifting, and all my secrets are floating to the surface, soon everyone will know about my dark passenger, my need to rape.*

CHAPTER 41

I KNOCKED ON CHIEF BURNS office door and entered, "You wanted to see me Chief?

"Please have a seat Officer Johnson, I need to get an update on where we are on the rape cases?"

"Did you get a chance to read my last report about the attempted robbery of Donna Jenkins?"

"Yes, I read it and I agree with you, that she could have very well been our next rape victim if the assailant hadn't been scared off. I know you haven't been on these cases very long, but have you developed any leads?"

"Yes, I have a couple of solid leads, for instance, all three victims described their assailant as being around 5 feet 6 inches tall and wearing a mask with rubber gloves during the attacks. They also described a small tattoo of a cross on the assailant left wrist. This leads me to believe that the same person committed all three rapes."

"You mentioned, last week, that you thought you recognize the tattoo from somewhere? Did you remember where?"

"No, it hasn't come to me yet, but it will sooner or later. I wish we could catch a break on these cases before this bastard rape someone else."

"Unfortunately, there was another rape last night. The victim was a Doctor Sara Moore, she was attacked at her own home between 10:30 and 11:30 last night."

"Dam, not another one?"

"Yes, I'm afraid so, but the big difference this time is that she was severely beaten. She's still alive, but she is in the hospital in pretty bad shape."

"So, he's escalating?"

"Yes, I believe he is.

"Has anyone interview Dr. Moore yet?"

"No, Officer Sherry Gross took the call, but said Dr. Moore was too incoherent to interview last night. I'd like for you to go to the hospital and see if you can get a statement from her."

"I assume that they didn't find any forensic evidence at Dr. Moore's house?"

"No, just like in the other cases, nothing was left behind, this guy's pretty smart.

That's all I have for now, if you turn up anything new, please let me know."

I left HQ and went to the hospital to get a statement from Dr. Moore. Her doctor gave me permission to speak with her, but only for a few minutes. I entered the room and saw how severely she had been beaten and had to choke back my tears. She was coherent enough to talk, but just barely.

The chief had explained to me my first day on the case that you have to go where the evidence leads you. I hadn't told him about my number one suspect for good reason, but Dr. Moore confirmed all my suspicions. The problem is I still need to find a way to prove it.

I finish-up at the hospital and drove to Dr. Moore's house where the rape had occurred. I wanted to look around for myself to see if something may have been missed.

I got out of my car and the weirdest thing happened, I seemed to be in a daze, and *I imagine that I could see the rapist run right past me, jump the two steps to the front porch and look inside the window.* It was almost like watching a scene from a movie and I was right in the middle of it.

I pulled on my rubber gloves, took down the yellow tape and unlock the front door with the keys that Dr. Moore had given me. She told me that she had heard a loud bang outside last night and went outside to investigate and that's when she was attacked.

I stepped back out on the porch to look for something that could have made the noise, but I didn't see anything. The only thing on the porch was two rocking chairs and a swing. Suddenly, I was in a daze again, and *I could see the rapist grabbing the porch swing and slamming it into the side of the house.*

I went back inside the house to look around and found myself in that daze again, *I could see the poor doctor lying on the floor with the rapist sitting on her stomach hitting her in the face again and again.* I felt a tear trickle down my cheek and picked up the phone to call the MSP forensics team. I asked them to come back to the crime scene because I wanted to be sure that they hadn't missed anything. They weren't happy about it but agreed to come anyway. *Maybe I was hoping for a miracle, but when you're going to accuse a cop of being a rapist you had better be dam sure you can prove it.*

CHAPTER 42

CHIEF BURNS RECEIVED A CALL from Duke's mother-in-law, "hello is this Chief Nick Burns?"

"Yes, speaking how can I help you?"

"This is Detective Duke Wayne's Mother-in-law. We've been trying to locate Duke since last night, do you have any idea where he is?"

"No, we don't, we've also been trying to reach him also but haven't been able to. Do you want me to give him a message if I see him before you do?" Chief Burns asked.

"Yes, please have him call me, I have some tragic news, Barbara, Duke's wife developed serious compilations last night at the hospital and despite their best efforts she didn't make it. Unfortunately, they weren't able to save the baby either."

"Oh my god, that's terrible, and Detective Wayne doesn't know?"

"We don't think so because we haven't been able to reach him. I spoke with the hospital about two hours ago and they told me they hadn't been able to reach him either."

"I'll head over there and if I can locate him, I'll have him call you right away," Chief burns replied.

"Thanks, I appreciate it."

Chief Burns hung up the phone and called Detective Thomas, "Dominick have you heard anything from Duke yet?"

"No, the last time I talked to him was yesterday afternoon, what the hell's going on?"

"I don't know yet, I'm heading to the hospital to look for Duke and I'll call you back shortly."

Chief Burns hung up the phone and quickly exited HQ. Placing his bubble light on the roof of the car, he drove to the hospital as fast as possible. Parking the car, he hurried across the parking lot, entered the sliding glass doors and rushed up to the information desk, "Can you please tell me if Officer Duke Wayne has been here?"

One of the ladies said, "Yes, he was here less than an hour ago and went to his wife's room."

"What's the room number?

"Well, it was 102," she replied.

Chief Burns hurried down the hallway looking for the correct room number. He saw a nurse and asked, "Has Detective Duke Wayne been here?"

"Yes, Mr. Wayne was here and spoke with Dr. George who told him the tragic news about his wife and baby. He was extremely upset and bewildered, when he left the hospital."

"Ok, thanks for the information, I appreciate it," Chief Burns replied.

Chief Burns went to the nurse's station and called Detective Thomas, "Dominick, I'm at the hospital and Duke's not here. His wife and baby died last night on the operating table. They informed him about it a little while ago, but nobody knows where he is right now. We need to find him he shouldn't be alone at a time like this. Can you go by his house to see if he went home and I'll go to HQ to see if he shows up there?"

"10-4, Chief, I'm on my way, I'm only a few blocks from his house."

Detective Thomas drove towards Duke's house wondering, *what he would say to him? He wished he could alleviate the terrible pain he must be feeling, but there are probably no words for that. The only thing he can do right now, is just be there for his partner.*

Detective Thomas saw Duke's car as he pulled into the driveway. He quickly climbed out of his car and ambled up the sidewalk knocking on the front door. Normally, he would open the door and walk on in, but it was locked.

"Duke unlock the door and let me in," it's Dominick.

"Go away Dominick, I'm OK, just leave me alone."

"Let me in Duke, you shouldn't be alone right now."

"Go away! Get the fuck out of here."

Detective Thomas went to the window and peered inside. Duke pick up a gun from the coffee table and Detective Thomas knew he had to do something fast. Going back to the front door, he bashed his shoulder into it, but it didn't budge. He bashed into it a second time and the door flew open slamming against the wall.

Detective Wayne was sitting on the couch in the living room and holding his gun up to the side of his head. Detective Thomas threw both hands up walking towards the couch. "Duke, what the fuck are you doing? Put down that gun, you don't want to go out like this man."

"Don't come any closer Dominick, I told you to get the fuck out of here."

"Duke you're my best friend and I'm not going anywhere. Now put that gun down," Dominick said as he tried to inch closer.

With tears streaming down his face he murmured, "You don't understand Dominick, I killed them, I killed them both, It's my fault their dead."

"What are you talking about Duke? Barbara died at the hospital and you had nothing to do with it. It's not your fault man, put down that gun." Dominick replied taking a step closer and thinking, *if he could just get close enough to grab the gun, he could wrestle it away from Duke.*

"The hospital called Barbara's Doctor last night and told her to get to the hospital right away. She told them she was on her way, but never arrived."

"Well, what the fuck does that have to do with you Duke, you're not making any sense?" Dominick said as he took a step closer.

"It all my fault, because last night when my wife was dying on the operating table, I was raping and beating the fuck out of her doctor."

"You're talking out of your head Duke, what you mean, you raped the doctor?"

"That's what I said, I raped her and they're dead because of me." Suddenly, Duke fired his 38 into the right side of his head and Detective Thomas dropped to his knees yelling, "No Duke, no."

It took several minutes for Detective Thomas to regain enough composure to get to his feet. With tears streaming down his face, he went to the end table, picked up the phone and called Chief Burns to tell him what had happened.

CHAPTER 43

CHIEF BURNS IMMEDIATELY got into his car and drove over to Duke's house dreading what he was about to see. He radioed Officer Faye-Lynn Johnson and asked her to meet him there. By the time Chief Burns and Officer Johnson arrived at the scene, the medical examiner was already there and ready to remove the body.

I entered the living room and saw the blood spattered on the wall and all over the side of the couch. I didn't know if I was going to throw up or cry. I reached up and wiped away a tear, trying not to get too emotional in front of everyone, but it was difficult. I had worked with Duke for a couple of years and he had helped me study for the Detectives exam, but he was also my number one suspect for the rapes.

Chief Burns and I approached Detective Thomas, "Can you tell us what happen Dominick?"

"When I got here, the front door was locked, and I had to bust it open. I came into the living room and Duke was sitting on the couch with a gun pointed to his head. I tried to talk him down, but he was talking crazy and wouldn't listen to me."

"What you mean he was talking crazy," Chief Burns asked.

"He said that he had beat-up and raped his wife's doctor last night, and that's why the doctor never showed up at the hospital to operate on Barbara. What kind of crazy shit is that?"

I reluctantly began to speak, "Dominick, there are some things that I need to tell you. Within the last twenty-four hours, Duke has developed into my number one suspect for the rapes. I'm sorry, I know he was your partner and friend, but we have a description from four women that matches Duke. We have a composite drawing of a tattoo that matches the one on his left wrist."

"I can't believe it, are you sure about this Faye-Lynn," Dominick asked.

"There's more, last night Barbara's doctor was beaten-up and raped. A few hours ago, when she woke up, I was able to get her statement. Although the rapist had a mask on, Dr. Moore recognized the attacker's voice immediately. Duke had been to her office at least a dozen times with his wife Barbara and she identified him as her attacker. Also, the forensic team got some fingerprints from the front porch swing, which places Duke at Dr. Moore's house.

I'm really sorry, at first I couldn't believe it either," I explained.

"He's been my partner for over two years, how could I have not known about him?" Dominick asked.

"I think he had us all fooled," the Chief replied.

An officer approached where we were standing and said, "Chief we found something in the basement you need to see."

We followed the Officer and made our way down the rickety steps into the dark, dirt floor basement. The Officer directed us over to a workbench near the back-right corner of the basement. Sitting on top of the workbench near the center was a small wooden box. The wooden box had etched carvings of what appeared to be naked women and a small gold latch.

Dominick and I watched as Chief Burns unhooked the gold latch and opened the wooden box. To our amazement, inside the box were seventeen small brown paper bags. The bags had the names and dates of girls that had been raped. Each bag contained a set of rubber gloves and a used condom. I know it's a little weird, but my first thought was, *I finally found the semen the rapist left behind, but seventeen, holly shit.*

A week later, I walked out of the funeral home thinking how sad it was that only ten people had showed up for Duke's funeral. The news of him being the rapist came out a few days before the funeral and I suppose that had a lot to do with the low turnout. I was there myself out of a sense of duty; after all he was still a police officer.

I'm happy that the rape cases are closed, but I'm not real sure what's in store for me next, *I guess the Chief will assign me back to my old squad. Is it too soon to say, that I'd love to have Duke's position? Na!*

CHAPTER 44

CHIEF BURNS SCHEDULED a meeting with Detective Thomas and me for 8:00 a.m., the day after the funeral. We entered his office and before we sit down, he asked us to accompany him back out into the squad room. There were around fifteen people in the squad room not counting us. Chief Burns yelled out, "Can I get everyone's attention."

Everyone quickly quieted down to see what was going on and Chief Burns said, "I'd like to introduce everyone to our newest Detective, Faye-Lynn Johnson."

He handed me a gold detective's shield and shook my hand congratulating me. Tears well-up in my eyes and I felt like hugging him, but I knew if I did the guys would never let me live it down. Everyone in the squad room acknowledge my promotion by clapping and yelling. Finally, Chief Burns said, "Ok, the party's over, let's get back to work."

Detective Thomas and I follow the Chief back into his office, he sat down at his desk and said, "please have a seat Detectives."

I sat down pulling out my note pad and my new partner looked at me and smiled. I didn't know if he was making fun of me for taking notes or just glad that he didn't have to.

"Faye-Lynn, I want you to work with Dominick on the lipstick murder cases. He can provide you with the case files and fill you in on all the details."

"Sure, no problem Chief, just so you know, I happened to be on all three of the crime scenes."

"That's great, that could prove to be very helpful." Chief Burns responded.

"Yes, I saw all the bodies plus I made some notes at each crime scene and turned them over to the detectives working the cases."

"You might want to dig them out if you still have them to insure, they were included in the reports. I've reviewed all the cases and there are a couple of things that I'd like to discuss with you. First let me say for the record that I think the same person or persons committed all three murders. I also think that we desperately need to identify the body found in the trunk at the watershed. I'm convinced that's the key to solving all the cases."

"I agree Chief," I alleged.

"With what Detective Johnson."

"With everything you just said," I replied.

Detective Thomas looked at me and gave me one of his big burley laughs. I decided from that point on that a new detective should be seen and not heard.

"There's something else that's been bugging me about the trunk. There's no mention of any vehicles in the reports and that trunk had to get there somehow. It was probably too big for a car, so we may be looking at a SUV, pick-up truck, or possibly even a van." Chief Burns explained.

"If there no mention of a vehicle in the reports, this isn't really a lead is it, Chief," Detective Thomas replied.

"Well, what I'd like you guys to do is to go back and interview the couple who found the trunk. We need to know if they saw a vehicle on the road while they were out walking that morning. Also, I want you to go to every house along that road and asked them about vehicles on the road that day or the night before.

"No problem Chief, we'll get right on it." Detective Thomas replied.

"Also, Detectives, in the second case at the shopping center, there were two persons of interest. I want you to interview them again."

"You want us to bring them in?" Detective Thomas asked.

"No that won't be necessary, just get their current address and go to their homes." Chief Burns stated.

"What if they asked why we're questioning them again?" Detective Thomas asked.

"Simply tell them we've discovered new information and we have reopened the case.

CHAPTER 45

SEAN BROOKS WAS WARMING a bowl of chili for dinner when suddenly there was the knock at the door. *Who in the fuck could that be? No one ever comes around here?*

He could feel his blood pressure spiking as he hurried over to the large cabinet on the wall. Reaching out, he quickly swung the doors shut hiding his treasure chest of pictures. There was another hard knock on the door as he walked towards it, "Who's there?"

"Frederick Police Department." Detective Thomas replied.

Sean could feel his heart hammering in his chest as he responded, "What do you want?"

"Could you please open the door? We need to talk to you."

Sean slowly opened the door and Detective Thomas and I stepped inside, "Hi, I'm Detective Johnson and this is my partner Detective Thomas."

"What do you want detectives?" Sean asked.

"We need to ask you a few questions about Stacy Rodgers, I understand that you knew her?" I asked.

"Yes, I considered her a close friend at the time of her death. What's going on? I answered all these questions years ago."

"We've discovered some new evidence and have reopened the case," Detective Thomas explained.

I was keeping a close eye on Mr. Brooks and watching every reaction. I noticed that his hands were shaking as he sat down at the kitchen table. I pulled out my notebook and asked, "How'd you and Stacy meet?"

"I was a Security Guard at the Shopping Mall where she worked. We became friends and I'd often stop by to talk to her. On the night she died I'd stopped by earlier in the evening and we talked for about ten minutes," Sean explained.

"What did you talk about?" I asked.

"Just bullshit," he replied.

"What kind of bullshit, Detective Thomas asked.

"I asked her to go on a date with me, but she turned me down."

"Did that piss you off?" Detective Thomas asked.

"No, it wasn't the first time that she'd turned me down."

"Then later you found her body in the storage room?" I asked.

"Yes," he replied and explained almost verbatim what he had told the detectives the night of the murder. I couldn't help but think, *it sounds to me like he has all this shit memorized.*

As Detective Thomas continued to question Mr. Brooks, I began to wander around thinking, *what a dump.* I walked toward the back of the trailer past an un-made bed and a large cabinet on the wall. I looked back towards the kitchen table where Sean was sitting, and Dominick seemed to have him well occupied with all the questions.

I glanced down and noticed a picture lying on the floor. Picking it up, I found myself staring at it intensely. I was in a daze, *and I could see two hands on her throat choking the life out of her,* Suddenly, I blurted out, "Who's this Sean?"

He quickly jumped up from the table and hurried over to where I was standing. He grabbed the picture from my hand and said, "She's a friend."

"It's not Stacy Rodgers, who is it?" I asked again.

The sweat was beading on his forehead he was turning pale and finely said "It's an old friend from high school."

"Well, what's your old friend's name." I asked.

"It was Sue Martin."

"Spell that for me," I replied as I wrote it in my notebook.

"Her name "was" Sue Martin, what did you mean by that?" I questioned.

"What, I don't understand your question?" Sean replied.

"A few seconds ago, when I asked you who was in the picture, you said her name "Was" Sue Martin. What do you mean, "was"? Is she dead or something?" I asked.

"What, no, no, I mean I don't know. We were close friends in high school, but I haven't seen her for years. I quit school my senior year to take care of my mother who had cancer and I never really saw much of Sue after that. Someone told me that she'd moved to Pennsylvania." Sean explained.

"If she "was" an old friend and you haven't seen her for years, why do you still have her picture?" I asked.

"Last time I checked Detective, it's not against the law to own a picture."

"You're right, it's not against the law, but it seems a little odd that this picture is lying here in the middle of the floor.

I mean you say you haven't seen her for years." I responded.

Mr. Brooks got a strange look on his face but didn't respond.

"I think we have enough for now, but we may need to come back for some follow-up questions at a later date." Detective Thomas chimed in.

"Look, I went through all this shit years ago when Stacy died, are you guys ever going to stop harassing me?" Sean asked.

Detective Thomas who stands around 6' 2" and weighs about 280, walked over to Sean, leaned over within an inch of his face and said, "No".

Sean tried his best to stay composed, but I knew we had shaking him. We left the trailer, climbed into our unmarked squad car and headed east.

"Did you see his reaction when you told him that we had re-opened the case? I thought he was going to shit his pants right then and there," I alleged.

"What about that picture? I thought he was going to kick your ass over that," Dominick said and let out one of his big burley laughs.

"What did he say her name was?"

"Sue Martin." I replied.

"We need to check her out, maybe interview her, to see what she can tell us about this guy." Dominick responded.

"What's our next move partner?" I asked.

"Let's go interview the couple who discovered the first body in the trunk.

"Sounds like a plan," I responded.

As we drove off, I couldn't help thinking, *how happy I was to finally be a detective.*

CHAPTER 46

THE DETECTIVES HAD LEFT more than an hour ago, but Sean Brooks was still pissed off. He rambled over to the side of the bed and lowered himself down on one knee. Reaching underneath the bed, he pulled out a plastic container and removed the lid.

Looking down at the journals stacked inside the container, he couldn't help thinking, *how glad he was, that he hadn't thrown them away.* He had tried to get rid of them the night he left for North Dakota, but he just couldn't force himself to do it. He wasn't sure why he wrote in the journals, only that it made him feel better.

The first time he wrote in a journal was the day his Mother died. He didn't have any friends and certainly couldn't talk to his Aunt, but he needed to explain to someone why he had killed her. After they took her body away that day, he sat down and just started to write. He explained every little detail and tried desperately to rationalize his actions.

Reaching down, he grabbed the journal from the top of the stack and carried it over to the kitchen table. This was the same journal he had been writing in since he had killed Tracy Roberts.

Opening the journal to a blank page, he began to write *today two pig detectives from the Frederick Police Department came to my trailer. They came to harass me about the murder of Stacy Rodgers. The female black chick was hot, but I could tell she was a fucking bitch. She would love to make a name for herself by nailing my ass to the wall, but that's never going to happen.*

The other detective was a big, ugly ass black guy. He got up in my face, but I could tell he was as dumb as a box of rocks. They're not going to catch me for the murder of Stacy Rodger's, Tracy Roberts's, Sue Martin's or even my mother, these pigs are just too fucking stupid.

I was a little worried when the black chick found my picture of Sue Martin lying on the floor. But as dumb as they are, I'm sure that nothing will ever come of it. After all, it has been nearly ten years since I put that bitch out of her misery those dumb bastards still haven't even identified her body. I'll keep my cool and outsmart these new detectives just like I have all the others.

Sean closed the journal, got up from the kitchen table and walked over to the side of the bed. Placing the journal back on top the stack, he closed the lid and pushed the container under the bed. He couldn't help thinking, *how dangerous it was to have the journals, if anyone ever discovered them that would be the end for him.*

Standing-up, he wandered to the far end of the bed, reached out and opened the two large cabinet doors that were hiding his pictures. Sitting on the edge of the bed, he began staring intently at the pictures. Glancing back and forth at Sue Martin, Stacy Rodgers and Tracy Roberts, he realized how much they all looked alike. They were all gorgeous with nice slender bodies, long beautiful blond hair and mesmerizing blue eyes. Suddenly, he murmurs, *no fucking wonder I fell in love with them, I only wish they would have loved me?*

A few days had passed since the detectives had visited Sean trailer to question him about Stacy Rodgers murder and he was still upset about it. As he was leaving work, he happened to notice an unmarked police car with tinted windows sitting in the parking lot and he could feel his rage building.

I closely watched as my suspect began to scurry across the parking lot towards his van and I pulled out my notebook to log the time. When I looked up from my notebook, he had turned away from his van and was quickly approaching my vehicle. He banged hard on my window and I slowly lowered it, but before I could say anything, he yelled, "What the fuck do you want Detective?"

I was all alone on the stakeout and felt very uncomfortable with the situation I had put myself into. I never really expected him to come on so strong. When we had questioned him a few days ago, he acted like a wimp, *talk about Dr. Jekyll and Mr. Hyde.*

After a few seconds I calmly looked up at him and stated, "good evening Mr. Brooks."

"Detective, this is harassment and I want you to stay the fuck away from me," he blurted out.

"Now Mr. Brooks, I can't do that, you're my number one suspect for the murder of Stacy Rodgers."

"Fuck you, he cried out, as he turned and quickly walked away.

CHAPTER 47

I PULLED OUT of the shopping mall following Sean's van and from the direction he was going I could tell he was heading home. I called Chief Burns on the radio and described what had just happened in the parking lot. He told me to call it a night, but I wanted to make sure my suspect was all tucked in.

Ten minutes later, Sean turned right off the main road and backed into his driveway. Shutting off his engine, he sat and watched as I slowly drove past. I went to the end of the street, turned around and came down the other side. I pulled to the curb and parked about twenty-five feet from the entrance of his driveway. From my location, I had a perfect view of him sitting in the driver's seat of the van staring at me. It was as if were waiting to see which one was going to blink first. After several minutes, he finally climbed out of the van and entered his trailer.

Sean slammed his keys down on the kitchen table *I don't want to deal with this fucking shit all over again.* He opened the cabinet doors to look at his pictures for a while. Whenever he was depressed, he would sit and stare at the pictures. In his twisted mind he thought about the imaginary connection that he still had with each of the women, *never-mind the fact that he had killed them.*

He sat on the edge of the bed and kicked off his shoes. Unbuttoning his shirt, he pitched it towards the clothes hamper. Turning off the lamp next to the bed, he stretched out on the bed and closed his eyes *he had to think.* I finally saw the light go out and waited around for another five or ten minutes to insure he was in for the night.

My partner and I had also gone back to interviewed Stacy Rodgers old boyfriend again, but my gut feeling is, *Sean Brooks is our guy, he killed her, we just need to figure out how to prove it.*

After lying in the dark for several minutes it suddenly came to Sean, I'm going to be smarter this time and turn the tables on the pigs. I'll follow them around *I need to find out why they reopened the Stacy Rodgers case and if they really have any new evidence.*

A few days after Sean had confronted Detective Johnson in the parking lot, he began to follow her. He sat outside the police station for nearly an hour waiting for her to exit the building. Finally, she came out with a female uniformed police officer around 5:10 p.m.

He waited and watched as they talked, *I know this bitch is out to get me, so I need to keep a close eye on her to see what the hell she's up to.* After a few minutes, Detective Johnson turned away from the other officer and hurried down the stairs of the HQ building. Crossing the street, she climbed into her unmarked vehicle and drove off.

Sean decided to let a few cars past before taking off to insure there was a safe distance between him and the detective. He wanted to stay far enough behind her that she wouldn't notice him on her tail.

Driving up North Market Street, Detective Johnson turned right onto Sixteenth Street. After passing a small shopping center, she went to the last house on the block and turned into the driveway. He quickly pulled over and parked a block up the street behind a large panel truck, so she couldn't see his van.

A few minutes later, she twisted out of her car and entered her house. It was a beautiful two-story colonial with a porch that stretched all the way across the front. He couldn't help but wonder, *how she could afford to live in this upscale neighborhood on a detective's salary.*

Sean sat and watched her house for a long time, he wanted to figure out if she was married or had a boyfriend. After almost two hours, no one entered or exited the house, so he begins to think *maybe there isn't anyone else.*

Getting bored, he decided it was time to go home. Starting the van, he drove off thinking, *tomorrow's another day and now I know where the bitch lives.*

CHAPTER 48

I PHONE THE RIDGEWAY'S to explain that we had re-opened the case of the un-identified body they'd discovered in 1982.

"Hello, is this Tom Ridgeway?"

"Yes, it is, how can I help you," he questioned.

"This is Detective Faye-Lynn Johnson, I'm not sure if you remember me, I know it's been a long time?"

"Sure, I remember, you were the first police officer to arrive the day we discovered the young girl's body in the trunk. So, you're a detective now, congratulations."

"Thanks, I appreciate it, the reason I'm calling, is to inform you that FPD has re-opened the case."

"Wow, after all this time?" he responded.

"Yes, we're taking a fresh look at the case and we'd like to set up an appointment to asked you a few follow-up questions."

"Well, Ellen and I are both retired now so we're pretty flexible, when did you want come by?" Mr. Ridgeway asked.

"Would Monday morning around 7:00 a.m. work for you?"

"That's fine see you then," he responded and hung up the phone.

Monday morning my partner and I left HQ early and were on our way to interview the Ridgeways. There were ten houses spread-out along the dirt road where the trunk had been discovered. According to the reports, the detectives who original worked the case had only interviewed the Ridgeways and the people where Ellen had called the police that morning. *I guess the detectives assume the other houses were too far away for them to know anything.*

I turned into the Ridgeways lane and pulled-up behind an old pick-up truck. It was full of dents and had primer paint spots all over it. I couldn't help but think *that looks like Fred Sanford truck.* Suddenly, my partner said, "nice looking truck," and I busted out laughing.

"What's so funny?" He asked.

"Never mind, I'll explained later, let's just go." I replied still grinning.

We exited the car and climbed the five stairs leading to the long front porch. I knocked on the door and Tom Ridgeway immediately swung it opened, "Hello detectives, please come in."

We enter the beautiful log cabin and sat down on a large blue couch that Mr. Ridgeway had directed us to. The Ridgeways sat across from us in two high back blue chairs and Ellen asked, "Can I offer you some coffee or something to drink."

My partner and I both declined.

I glanced around the log cabin and I could see striate into the kitchen from where I was sitting. There were white cabinets with black granite counter tops and stainless-steel appliances. The living room had a gorgeous stone fireplace with a large bearskin rug scatter out in front of it. I began to drift away and could see myself lying on the bearskin rug in my black negligee, with a glass of wine, waiting for some hunk to make his next move.

Suddenly, I snapped back to reality and found myself feeling a little uncomfortable, time to get back to business.

"This is Detective Thomas and as you know I'm Detective Johnson. As I mention to you on the phone, we've re-opened our investigating and would like to ask you a few questions."

"Sure, go ahead detective, we're happy to help if we can." Mr. Ridgeway replied.

"When you were out walking the day you discovered the trunk, did you see anyone else?" I asked.

Mr. Ridgeway shook his head and replied, "No, we didn't see anyone."

"From the time you started walking until the time you discovered the trunk, did any vehicles pass you on the road," Detective Thomas asked.

"No, we don't get a lot of traffic up here," Ellen, explained.

"How about the night before, did you hear anything unusual during the night." I asked.

"We were in bed by 11:00 and didn't hear any vehicle's or anything unusual that night," Tom replied.

We asked several more questions before I thanked them for their time, and we left. My partner and I had previously agreed to keep our interview short and to the point knowing that the Ridgeways had been interviewed many times throughout the years.

"Do you think we learned anything new Dominick?" I asked as we climbed into the car.

"Not really, but they did confirm a few things that were in the original reports and I think that's helpful."

"So, what's next?" I asked.

"Next we interview everyone else who lives on this road."

As I pulled out of the Ridgeway's lane I explained, "there's a house about a half mile up the road. It's where Ellen called the police the morning, they discovered the body. I think we should go there first and then we can work our way back to interview the others."

"Sounds like a plan," my partner replied letting out one of his big burley laughs.

We arrived at the first house and our interview only lasted about five minutes. The homeowners had bought the house less than a year ago and were not in the area in 1982.

Turning the car around, I started going the other way and drove about two miles past the Ridgeway's stopping at the next house. We questioned the occupants and one by one continued to the other houses scatter along the road. I was getting frustrated and told my partner, "I think we're wasting our time."

"We've already completed eight of the ten interviews, let's just finish these last two. Then we can tell the Chief that we interviewed every possible witness."

"10-4?" I responded.

We arrived at the next house and I noticed that some extra trees had been cleared at the end of the lane creating a small pull-off area on the main road. The house was a beautiful log cabin with a big picture window to the right of the front door and a single window to the left.

I led the way up the stairs to the front porch and knocked on the door. It slowly opened and standing before us was a short man just over five feet tall with grey hair. "Hello, I 'm detective Johnson and this is my partner Detective Thomas. We'd like to ask you a few questions about the body discovered a few miles up the road back in 1982?"

The man introduced himself as Jack Toms and said, "Sure, I remember that like it was yesterday. There was a lot of people running around up here in the mountain that day."

"We just have a few questions if you don't mind? I replied.

"Sure, no problem."

"Has anyone ever questioned you about this before?" I asked.

"Nope, but we do live a good way from where the body was discovered, so I wasn't really surprised," he replied.

"Did you or your wife see or hear anything unusual or suspicious that morning," Detective Thomas asked.

"No, not really."

"What about the night before?" I asked.

"Well, there was something, I got up around 2:30 to use the bathroom and I heard a vehicle pull over on the main road at the end of my lane. I looked out the window and saw a white van pulled over on the side of the road."

"Wait, did you say a white van," I confirmed.

"Yes.

"What happen next," my partner asked.

"I thought maybe it was kids just looking for a place to take a leak and it scare me at first, but I never saw anyone get out of the van. After a few minutes it pulled off and I went back to bed. The following day they found the body and my wife told me I should report what had happened the night before, but I never did.

"Why not," I asked?

"If someone would have come by to question me, I probably would have mentioned it, but they didn't, so I didn't think it was all that important," he responded.

We asked Mr. Toms several more questions and thanked him for his help.

As I hurried into the car, I was feeling an adrenaline rush.

"Did you hear what he said about the white van? Guess who else drives a white van?" I blurted out to my partner?

"Who?" Detective Thomas inquired, feeling confident he already knew the answer.

"Our suspect for Stacy Rodger's murder, Sean Brooks"

"That's a leap isn't its Faye-Lynn, this murder was back in 82?" Detective Thomas questioned.

"Maybe, maybe not," I responded.

We stopped to interview the family at the last house on the dirt road but were only there a few minutes. The homeowners didn't have much to offer, they had been out of town on vacation when the body was discovered.

CHAPTER 49

WE SCHEDULED A MEETING for Tuesday morning with Chief Burns to brief him on the status of our investigation. Dominick tapped lightly on the opened glass door as we entered the Chief's office.

"Morning Chief," I said as I trailed in behind my partner.

"Good morning guys, please have a seat."

"Chief, we interviewed Sean Brooks on Saturday about the Stacy Rodgers murder like you asked," my partner explained.

"How that go, did we learn anything new?" Chief Burns asked.

I tried hard, but I couldn't hold myself back any longer and blurted out, "I think this guy's guilty as hell, he knows a lot more than he is telling us." *Did I just say that, I asked myself, but it was too late, I was jumping to conclusions without any evidence, a rookie mistake?*

"What are you basing that on Faye-Lynn?" the Chief asked.

"Well for one thing, when I mentioned that we had re-opened the Stacy Rodgers murder case, it was clear that he was rattled."

"That's not evidence, do we have anything else on this guy," the Chief asked.

"I found a picture lying on the floor which seemed out of place. I picked it up and had to do a double take. It was a beautiful young blonde who resembled Stacy Rodgers, but it wasn't her. He was upset when he realized I'd found the picture and quickly approached me jerking it from my hand."

"Were you able find out who it was?" the Chief asked.

"Yes, but I had to asked him several times before he finally gave me a straight answer. He said her name was Sue Martin, an old friend from high school."

"Well, what's so usually about a picture of an old friend," the Chief asked.

Dominick finally spoke-up, "something doesn't add up for us Chief, Mr. Brooks said that he hadn't seen the girl in the picture since high school, so why would it be lying there on the floor. There was a cabinet on the wall I suppose the picture could have fallen out of it, but the doors were closed and locked."

"The girl in the picture was way too attractive to be friends with that looser, he was probably stalking her," I added, getting an unfamiliar scowl from the Chief.

"Let's not jump the gun here Faye-Lynn, but I do think you may be on to something. Let's try to locate this Sue Martin to see what kind of connection she has to Mr. Brooks," the Chief ordered.

"Chief, we also went back to the watershed where the trunk was discovered with the first victim. We interviewed someone from each of the ten houses along the road starting with the Ridgeways who had discovered the body," I explained.

"Did you get anything new?" the Chief asked.

"We didn't get any new leads from the Ridgeways, but we were able to confirm several things that were on the original reports. We also talked to a Mr. Jack Toms who described hearing a noise outside his cabin around 2:30 the morning the day the body was discovered. He went to a window to investigate and saw a white van with the motor running sitting at the end of his lane. No one exited the van and after a few minutes it pulled off," Dominick explained.

"Was Mr. Toms able to get a tag number?" the Chief asked.

"No, the van was sitting at the wrong angle for him to see the front or rear of the van," I explained.

"That's too bad, that could have been a great lead?" the Chief responded.

"Chief, I know it was a long time ago when Mr. Toms saw the van, but you know who else drives a white van," I asked with a hint of excitement.

"Who," Chief Burns responded.

"Sean Brooks, our suspect in the Stacy Rodger's murder case." I responded.

"That's may be just a coincidence, but I'd like you to go-back and review the statements from the two homeless men in the Tracy Roberts case. I thought that they had also mentioned something about a white van." Chief Burns alleged.

"If that's true we may have a link to all three cases," I blurted out.

"You could be right Faye-Lynn, that's all for now and thanks for the update," the Chief said.

Two hours later I knocked on Chief's Burns door and entered, "you got a minute Chief."

"Sure, come on in Faye-Lynn, what's up?"

"Chief, I think we have a break in this case."

"That's great Faye-Lynn, what-you-got?

"I ran a background check on Sue Martin and found out that her last known address was 226 Culler Avenue, Frederick Md. Also, we finally received a list of dental students from the schools in Pennsylvania. I was combing through them and you'll never believe who was on one of the lists," I alleged pausing for effect.

"Are going to tell me or not?" the Chief asked breaking into a smile.

"Sue Martin, I saw her name and couldn't believe it. I called the Director of the program and he said that she was one of his better students but had dropped out. She was in a two-year dental program in York Pennsylvania but quit after only a year. According to his records, the last class that she attended was August 22, 1982."

"This is all very interesting Faye-Lynn, but where are going with it?"

"Chief, I remembered that the Jane Doe discovered in the trunk at the watershed had extensive dental work done by an amateur. I confirmed with the Director that the school allowed students to work on each other and that a student had in fact done dental worked on Sue Martin."

"How in the hell did you remember something like that?"

"It's in the ME's report, I've read it several times and I believe Sue Martin is our Jane Doe. Sean Brooks admitted he was friends with Sue Martin in high school and we also know he was friends with Stacy Rodgers, he's our killer, I can feel it my gut."

"This is great work Faye-Lynn, but we're not there yet, send the dental records over to the FBI to compare with our Jane Doe. You and Detective Thomas check out Sue Martin's last known address. If you knock on her door and she answers, we're all going to look like idiots, so for now, let's just keep this between us."

"Understood," I said as I turned and quickly headed for the bullpen to look for my partner. I could feel the adrenaline rush in my stomach, and it was awesome.

CHAPTER 50

SEAN BROOKS SURVEYED as the two detectives exited FPD's headquarters building. He was determined to find out what the hell they were up to and had been waiting for nearly two hours. *Why had they re-opened the Stacy Rodgers murder case, had they really discovered new evidence and even more important am I in danger.*

Crossing the street, they climbed into their unmarked police vehicle and quickly drove off. Sean slowly worked his way into the traffic trying to avoid any unnecessary attention. Keeping a safe distance, he followed the detectives up North Market Street and down West Seventh Street. "Where in the hell are you pigs going," he whispered to himself.

Suddenly they turned right onto Culler Avenue. He had a strange tingling sensation in his left hand and his chest was pounding so hard he could feel the thumping in his head. He thought he was having a heart attack.

The detectives had stopped directly across the street from where Sue Martin the love of his life had once lived. He pulled over nearly a block down the street where he could observe them without being seen. *"What the fuck are they doing here,"* he wondered. *Had they figured out after all these years that the body in the trunk was Sue Martin's, they must have, why else would they be here?"*

Exiting their vehicle, the detectives sauntered up the sidewalk to Sue Martin last known address. Stepping up on the porch, Detective Thomas reached out and rang the doorbell. "I'm going to be pretty dam surprise if Sue Martin answers this door," I lean over and whispered to my partner.

"I agree Faye-Lynn, but maybe whoever lives here now can give us a lead or something to go on."

After several minutes an older gentleman opened the front door.

"Hi, I'm Detective Johnson and this is my partner Detective Thomas."

"I'm William Hatfield, but my friends call me Bill, what's this all about"

I showed Bill a picture of Sue Martin that the dental school had provided me and asked, "Do you know this girl?"

"Nope, never seen her before," he replied.

"How long have you lived here?" My partner asked.

"Since September of 84, I bought the house at a tax sale. The guy from the bank told me the house had been abandoned. It was full of old furniture and junk that I had to get rid of, before I could move in," he responded.

"What you'd do with all the stuff?" I asked.

"I took most of it to the landfill, but I did keep a few of the antique pieces. I was going to fix them up to sell, but never got around to it. I can show them to you if you want."

"Yes, I'd think we'd like to take a quick look if you don't mind," I responded.

Bill led the detectives around the side of the house and Sean tried to submerge himself lower into the front seat. He imagined that the detectives were gazing down the street towards him and he wished that he could just disappear. They walked towards an old shed in the back yard and Bill pulled some keys from his pocket unlocking the double doors. "The sheds sixteen by twenty and one of the reasons I bought the place," Bill proudly stated.

The detectives were inside the shed now and out of Sean's line of sight. He couldn't help but wonder, *what the hell they were looking for?*

Switching on the light, Bill ambled to the rear of the shed and pulled back a large blue tarp. Underneath it was two beautiful antique dressers and a coffee table with a broken glass top.

Approaching one of the dressers, I began to open each drawer hoping something had been left behind, but every drawer was completely empty not even a mothball. I was getting frustrated, but when I opened the very last drawer, there in the right-hand corner was a set of false teeth impressions. Bill laughed and said, "I thought I had thrown them away years ago."

I removed a pair of rubber gloves from my jacket pocket and pulled them on. Lowering myself down, I picked up the teeth impressions to get a closer look. I flipped them over and, on the bottom, etched in very small print was the name Sue Martin.

"Dominick can you get me some evidence bags from the car?"

"Sure, I'll be right back."

Sean watched as the big detective ambled through the side yard towards his car. He opened the trunk removing something and then hurried back to the shed. Dominick held open a plastic baggie as I dropped the teeth impressions inside sealing it. He began looking through the second dresser but didn't find anything.

I lowered myself down to inspect the coffee table and could see several small brown spots on the shard glass around the edges. Clutching my service revolver from my holster and holding it by the barrel, I tapped down hard on the glass. "Hey, what the hell you think you doing?" Bill asked with a frown on his face.

"Collecting evidence, there's something brown on the glass and I need to get it checked out."

I squatted down picking up the glass particles that I had broken out and dropped them inside another baggie. We then place the evidence into two separate paper bags and thanked Bill for his help. We asked him to hold onto the furniture a little longer just in case our forensic experts wanted to come back to examine it.

Dominick waited for Bill to get out of earshot, and then asked, "What's up with the glass on that coffee table Faye-Lynn, it just looked dirty to me?"

"You remember the trunk up at the watershed?" I asked.

"Yeah, what about it?"

"There were a few glass particles found inside the trunk and a few embedded in the victim's clothing. I'm going to send these samples to the FBI lab to see if they match the glass in the trunk."

"I think you're really reaching, Faye-Lynn?"

"Just a hunch."

"Dam girl, you're starting to scare me, you sound like a real detective."

"Put the evidence in the trunk you big lug." I said laughing as we headed off towards our car.

Sean watched as the detectives approached the car and noticed that the big guy was carrying two brown paper bags. He opened the trunk and placed the bags inside. *What the fuck could they possibly have in those bags after all these years,* he asked himself as he wiped the sweat from his forehead.

CHAPTER 51

"WE SHOULD INTERVIEW some of the neighbors before we head back to HQ Dominick."

"I agree, where do you want to start."

"Over there I guess," I responded and pointed towards the house on the South side of Sue Martin old house.

I knocked on the door and a very attractive lady with dark hair and brown eyes answered the door. She was wearing jeans, a white t-shirt with no bra and I couldn't help but envy her perky little breasts.

"Hi, I'm Detective Johnson and this is my partner Detective Thomas."

"How can I help you detectives?"

I showed her the picture of Sue Martin and asked, "Have you ever seen this girl before?"

"No."

"Are you sure she lived next door?" I asked.

"I'm sure, I moved here a year ago and Bill Hatfield was living there," she replied.

"Thanks, we appreciate your help," my partner replied.

We walked away from the first house and my partner said, "We may be wasting our time Faye-Lynn, Sue Martin hasn't lived here for a long time."

"Let's at least interview the neighbor over here, someone had to have known this young girl," I said walking towards the house.

I stepped-up on the front porch and knock on the door. After a few minutes an older lady wearing glasses, with bleach blonde hair answered the door. "Hi, I'm Detective Johnson and this is my partner Detective Thomas," I said, flashing my badge.

"Please to meet you, I'm Ruth Bowers." She gazed at me for a few seconds and said, "you're cute, I didn't know they let girls on the police force."

"Yes, it's true, I've been on the force for over twelve years now."

"You don't say," she replied.

I showed Mrs. Bowers the picture of Sue Martin and asked, "Do you recognize this girl."

"Of course, I know her, that's little Sue Martin, she used to live right next door. Bill Hatfield lives over there now, he's not a very nice person."

"Well, I'm sorry to hear that, but it's important that we locate Sue Martin, do you have any idea where she moved to?" I replied.

"No, I use to talk to her all the time, and it was the weirdest thing, one day she was just gone. She never told me goodbye or anything. Bill told me she left everything behind, lots of clothes and all her furniture."

"Did you file a missing person's report?" My partner asked.

"Oh no, I just assumed she'd moved to York, Pennsylvania where she was going to school. She often talked about getting a place up there, she hated the commute."

"Did you ever see anyone else at Sue's house like family or friends?" I asked.

"She did have a boyfriend at one point, but she had broken up with him a couple of months before she left. I talked to him a few times when they were out in the yard. His name was Tim Main and he seemed like a real nice boy.

"You've been very helpful Mrs. Bowers, if you think of anything else please give me a call," I explained handing her one of my new business cards.

"You don't think something bad has happened to Sue, do you?"

"We're not sure, that's why we're trying to locate her, thanks again Mrs. Bowers," my partner replied.

Sean watched as the two detectives exited the house, climbed into their unmarked vehicle and drove off. He felt like he was in a state of shock and couldn't move. He had a terrible headache and felt an awful thumping in his chest. Glancing down, he had been gripping the steering wheel so tight that his knuckles had turned white.

In the last twelve years, the police had followed, questioned, intimated and harassed him but they had never gotten this close. They'd had reopen the Stacy Rodger's case and now they were hot on the trail of what happened to Sue Martin.

He sat for several minutes mulling everything over in his head realizing that he was in trouble. *My neat little world of lies is crumbling all around me and I have no one to talk to. I need to try to act normal act like nothing's wrong if I'm going to survive.*

CHAPTER 52

MY PARTNER SCHEDULED a meeting for Wednesday morning with Chief Burns to bring him up to speed on the latest interviews we had conducted. We entered his office at 9:00 a.m. sharp. "Good morning detectives, please have a seat," the Chief said pointing towards two chairs facing his desk.

I sat down and jump right into it, almost rambling, "Chief, we went to 226 Culler Ave, which was Sue Martin's last known address. She no longer lives there and seems to have disappeared around the same time the body was discovered at the watershed. William Hatfield bought her house in September of 84 in a tax sale. Mr. Hatfield explained to us that the house was full of old clothes and furniture when he bought it. He had gotten rid of most of the stuff but kept a couple of old dressers and a coffee table."

"Did you get a chance to take a look at any of the stuff he kept?" The Chief asked.

"Yes, he had stored the stuff in an old shed behind his house and volunteer to show it to us. We looked through the dressers and I discovered a set of teeth impressions with Sue Martin's name on them. The coffee table had a broken top and near the edge I found some brown spots on the shard glass. I thought the spots could be blood, so we collected some samples and sent them over to the FBI crime lab."

"How long before we get the test results back?" The Chief asked.

"I asked them to put a rush on it and Chandra Diggs called me this morning. She said that the glass partials from the coffee table are a positive match to the glass that was found in the trunk in 1982. She also confirmed that Sue Martin's dental records obtained from the dental school in Pennsylvania are a positive match to our Jane Doe."

"Did anyone every file a missing person's report on Sue Martin?" The chief asked.

"No, we interviewed her foster parents and they said she had no real relationship with them. They hadn't spoken with her since her eighteen birthdays when she moved out. Her neighbor, Ruth Bowers believed that she had moved to York, Pennsylvania where she was going to school," Dominick explained.

"Chief, I think this confirms that Sean Brooks has a connection to at least two of our victims and we'd like to get a search warrant for his trailer," I explained expecting some push back.

"I agree, I'll go to the courthouse to present our evidence tomorrow, which means it could be as late as Friday before I actually get a warrant.

Chief Burns dismissed the detectives, so he could began working on his presentation for Judge Tisdale describing the evidence that they had collected. He knew getting a search warrant to look inside a suspect's home could be critical to solving any case. Of course, it's always a possibility that the search doesn't turn up any new evidence, but he believed that they are dealing with a serial killer and they like to keep trophies.

CHAPTER 53

A FEW DAYS HAD PASSED since the two detectives questioned Sue Martin's neighbors, but they hadn't been back to question him. *What could that mean, can my life get back to normal or is it changed forever, the worst part is not knowing.*

Sean knew he couldn't follow both detectives, so he'd decided to follow the hot black chick, Detective Johnson. She exited police headquarters just after five o'clock with a stack of files under her arm. He watched as she went to the passenger side of the vehicle, opened the car door and placed the files on the front seat.

Climbing into the driver's side she drove off and Sean pulled out a few cars behind. Up ahead, he could see her car when she turned into the subdivision and he followed. She drove a few more blocks and now they were on her street. Her house was the last one on the left and Sean watched as she turned into her driveway. Retrieving the files from the passenger seat, she quickly entered the house.

Sean had parked at his usual spot up the street behind a big panel truck where he couldn't be seen from the Detective's house. He glanced at his watch and it was five-twenty already, he had to be at work by six. He was already dressed in his Security Guard's uniform, which included the web belt that he hated so much. It never seems to stay up, but he needed a way to carry his handcuffs, flashlight, nightstick and his service weapon.

After watching the house for about twenty minutes, Sean started the Van and was about to leave when suddenly, Detective Johnson came out of the house. She scrambled into her car, backed out of the driveway and was coming strait towards him. He quickly ducked down in the seat as she went flying by.

Seating up, he wiped the sweat from his forehead on his shirtsleeve hoping she hadn't noticed him. *This is the perfect opportunity to break into her house,* he thought, but he couldn't move, he sat there for another twenty minutes going back and forth with himself. *I need to know what's in those files, but it could be dangerous what if she returns. If I can just get past those first two houses, I could be home free, but what if one of the neighbors sees me going towards her house, maybe I should just go to work and forget the whole thing.*

He suddenly heard a familiar voice in his head, his Mother's, "Get the fuck out of there now Sean?"

My mother was the only one who ever really knew me and loved me since she's been gone, I've felt so alone. This is one of those moments when I wish I was like everyone else and I'd know exactly what to do. I crave control of my own destiny and I'm not just going to stand by waiting for something to happen.

Sean jumped out of the van and began jogging down the street towards the detective's house. He continued past the front of the house to the far side, so he could circle around to the back. When he turned the corner, he noticed a six-foot high cedar fence surrounding an oval swimming pool.

Climbing over the fence, he began looking for a way to break into the house. He approached a single door to the right, tried the knob and it was locked. He then went over to a set of double doors to the left and they were also locked.

Pulling a penknife from his pocket he opened a straight slot screwdriver blade. Turning the doorknob as far as it would go, he jammed the screwdriver in between the two doors. He then smashed his shoulder hard against the doors and the right door popped open.

Entering the house, he found himself in the family room located just off the kitchen. There was a big fireplace with two large gray chairs facing towards it. On the other side of the room was a couch that matched the chairs with two end tables, but the files were nowhere in sight. Turning to his right, he wiped the sweat from his forehead and looked towards the kitchen counter tops, *no files*.

He made his way down the long hallway to the raised foyer, turned left and headed upstairs. Reaching the top of the stairs, he turned right into a large bedroom. It was neat and looked as if no one had ever slept there. Opening the door to the hall bath, he took a quick glance inside. Finally, he entered the master bedroom and there lying on the edge of the bed were the case files he so desperately wanted to see.

Approaching the edge of the bed, he picked up the top file and began to read Sue Martin case file. His chest was hurting, and the sweat was dripping from the side of his face as he glanced through the other files. A sick feeling came over him, *I've never thought about the future about growing old, maybe because the future has never been kind to people like me.*

CHAPTER 54

CHIEF BURNS RECEIVED a call from Judge Tisdale asking him a few questions about the request for the search warrant. He then informed the Chief that he was approving the warrant and it could pick-it-up around 5:30.

The Chief drove to the courthouse and parked in the reserved spot for the police department. Rushing out of the car, he glanced at his watch as he ambled up the stairs. Pulling open one of the huge double wooden doors he stepped inside and approached the information desk. There was an attractive young brunette behind the counter reading a magazine. "Hi, I'm Chief Nickolas Burns, did Judge Tisdale leave a search warrant here for me?"

"No, let me call his office," picking up the phone, she pushed a button on the switchboard and said, "Chief Burns is here to pick up a search warrant."

"Please have a seat over their Chief, Judge Tisdale's clerk will be right out," she said hanging up the phone.

A few minutes later, someone exited from one of the large oak doors that lined the hallway of the historic courthouse building. He approached the Chief and said, "Hi, I am Jake Efland, Judge Tisdale's law clerk, he asked me to deliver this to you."

"Thanks, I appreciate it and thank the Judge for me," the Chief said as he turned to leave.

Chief Burns had asked the Detectives and uniforms to meet him back at HQ at six o'clock. Everyone huddled in the parking lot as the Chief read the search warrant to make sure everyone knew what was covered.

Getting into his car, Chief Burns pulled out of HQ's parking lot and after driving a few blocks merged onto route fifteen towards Sean Brook's trailer park. The uniforms were in the two cars behind him and my partner and I were bringing up the rear. As we got closer and closer to Sean Brooks trailer park, I could feel the adrenaline rush and it was an amazing feeling.

A few minutes later Chief Burns swung into the empty driveway beside the trailer. The other cars stop in all different directions blocking the street. The uniforms quickly secured the area around the trailer. My partner and I exited our vehicle and approached the trailer door.

Dominick knocked on the door several times calling out, "Frederick Police Department, open up."

After a few minutes I turned to Chief Burns and said, "he's probably working, I think he goes in around six o'clock."

"Ok, open it, he doesn't have to be here for us to execute the search warrant," Chief Burns replied.

Dominick took a crowbar and wedged the door open within seconds. I entered the trailer and headed straight for the large cabinet hanging on the wall. The two doors were closed and locked, but this is where I had previously discovered the picture of Sue Martin lying on the floor and I had to see what else was inside.

Dominick quickly ripped the latch from the wood with his crowbar and I swung both doors wide open and blurted out, "Holy shit, Chief, you've got to see this."

He walked over, and we couldn't believe what we were seeing. There were hundreds of pictures on the inside of the cabinet. Pictures of Sue Martin, Tracy Rodgers, and Stacy Roberts.

"Here's our connection to the third victim Chief," I said as I shook my head back and forth in disbelief.

"I think your right Faye-Lynn," he responded.

"I wonder, *who the pictures of the older women are?*" I mumble.

"Could be his mother, he told us when we interviewed him that she died of cancer in 78," Dominick replied.

"We'll need to ask him that when we throw the cuffs on him," I replied.

"Dominick, you notice anything weird about the pictures?"

"What you mean, that the girls all kind-of resemble each other? He asked.

"Yes, not only that, but they all resemble the older woman too."

"Dam, I think your right partner," he replied.

I finally pulled myself away from the pictures and began searching the kitchen cabinets. Dominick had searched the dressers and I asked, "Did you find anything partner."

"Just some old dirty underwear," he replied busting out in to one of his big burleys laughs.

I opened a small closet door discovering a winter coat and four Security Guard uniforms. Sliding the hangers to the left, I noticed an old red sweater. It had several holes in it and some buttons were missing.

I wasn't surprise by the condition of the sweater, because if it was the one, I was looking for it was at least twelve years old. I removed it from the hanger, turned to one of the uniforms and asked, "Would you please bag this."

The trailer was so small that in less than ten minutes we were running out of places to look. I pulled my miniature flashlight from my pocket and approached the left side of the bed. Crouching down on one knee I shined the light under the bed and discovered several storage containers. My first thought was, *perfect, I've probably discovered more dirty underwear.*

Sliding one of the container's out from under the bed, I removed the lid and looked inside. There was a spiral ring notebook with big bold black letters, which spelled out Journal # 4. Underneath the lettering, was a set of lips drawn and colored with red ink. I opened the journal and began to read, "Oh My God! Chief, we hit the mother lode."

I grabbed the second journal and quickly scanned through it, then the third. "What the hell are they Faye-Lynn? Are you going to tell us or not?" The Chief asked.

"They're handwritten details of the lipstick murders and the first journal is all about him killing his own mother." I explained.

"We got him," Dominick said with a hint of excitement."

"Don't get me wrong there is a-lot-of other bull-shit in them, but they are also written confessions of each murder," I explained.

We carefully removed the pictures and the journals, putting them into evidence bags. We exited the trailer and Chief Burns instructed the uniforms to go back to headquarters and help him log in all the evidence that we had collected.

"Detective Thomas I need you to head over to the shopping mall where Sean Brooks works and pick-up surveillance on him. Keep an eye on him tonight and Faye-Lynn can relieve you first thing tomorrow morning. Detective Johnson you go on home and get some rest. I'm going to ask Judge Tisdale to issue a bench warrant for his arrest, but it may take a day or two. Until we make an arrest, I want someone on him twenty-four/seven."

I dropped my partner off at HQ to pick-up another vehicle and headed home. I couldn't help wondering, *why Sean Brooks had killed his own Mother and if that was his trigger to kill these young girls.*

Detective Thomas called Chief Burns on the radio at 7:35, "Chief I'm at the shopping mall and Sean Brooks didn't show up for work tonight. His supervisor said he didn't call in sick very often and that he hardly ever misses work."

"Go back to the trailer Detective, he has to show up there sooner or later."

"10-4, I'll check-in once I get there, but I'd like to swing by Faye-Lynn's first. I tried calling her, but I didn't get an answer. She should be home by now and I want to make sure everything's ok."

"What you mean Detective?"

"She asked me not to say anything to you, but she thought she saw Sean Brooks following her the other day. She thought it was kind-of-funny, but I think he's dangerous. He's confronted her once and until we have eyes on him, I think she might be in danger."

"Do you want me to send back up?"

"I don't think that'll be necessary, but I just need to check it out for my own peace of mind.

"I agree it's better to be safe than sorry Dominick."

CHAPTER 55

SEAN BEGAN TO GATHER up the files when suddenly, he heard a car pull into the driveway. He dropped the files back on the bed and tried to re-arrange them like he'd found them. Hurrying over to the front window he peaked through the blinds and could see the hot black detective climbing out of her car.

"Fuck," there wasn't time for him to get back downstairs and escape out the back door. He looked around the room and began to panic, he was trapped, and he knew it. *This is how Custer must have felt surrounded. Life is so fragile, every breath could be your last, nothing last forever, and eventually most killers get caught.*

He noticed a large closet on the other side of the room, with two bi-fold doors. He scampered over to the closet as fast as he could, stepped inside and closed the folding doors. He could hear the detective who was in the house now moving around down stairs. She walked across the hardwood floor and he could hear every tormenting step thumping in his head.

She threw her keys on the kitchen counter making a smacking sound and then more steps across the hardwood. Suddenly, he heard footsteps coming up the stairs and every step seemed to get louder and louder. Trying not to make a sound he reached up and wiped the sweat from his eyebrows.

Peering through the center crack of the bi-fold doors, he watched as Detective Johnson entered the bedroom. Walking to the side of the bed, she removed her holster from her belt and laid it on the nightstand. Sitting on the edge of the bed, she glanced down at the files and noticed they were no longer in the neat little pile that she had laid them in. *They must have slid around when she sat down,* she thought as she began to unbutton her blouse.

Standing up, she removed her blouse and bra and tossed them on the bed. Sean couldn't help thinking about, *how hot she was, another place another time he would be pretty turned on right now. Even though she was a cop, which I hate, she has a gorgeous body.*

She pulled down the zipper on the side of her slacks and let them fall to the floor. Bending over, she picked them up and threw them on the bed with the other clothes. Every now and then he would let out a breath of air, not even realizing he had been holding it.

He supposed that she was getting ready to jump in the shower and he began to reason, *when she goes into the bathroom, I can escape. I'll go down the stairs and out the front door, that's the shortest route. Just a few more minutes and I can get the fuck out of here.*

The detective sauntered around the edge of the bed but instead of going into the bathroom she headed to the closet where he was hiding. *Time to deviate from the plan, it may be ill advised, but sometimes you just don't have a choice.*

I folded back the bi-fold doors to my closet and saw a man, a killer standing in my closet and I began to scream. He reached out with both hands, grabbing me around the neck and started to squeeze. His hands were so strong they felt like vice grips around my neck and they seemed to be getting tighter and tighter.

I was in shocked and began falling backwards towards the bed. As astonished and weak as I felt, I knew I had to fight back. If I land backwards on the bed, he will have the momentum in his favor and he's going to kill me. He pushed me backwards towards the bed and I came up with my right knee to his testicles. He folded over, but only for a second, then he started coming at me again.

I began to catch my breath and said, "Sean you're fucking with the wrong woman. I'm no hundred- and twenty-pound teenager like the other girls you've killed or your mother, you sick fuck."

He began to laugh and said, "Denial is the first stage of the grieving process, when you know you're going to die."

Lunging forward, he tried to grab me around the throat again, but I was able to side step and punch him in the jaw knocking him backwards.

I turned away from him and quickly headed towards the nightstand where I had placed my weapon. He caught me from behind grabbing a handful of hair throwing me backwards onto the bed. In a split second, he was on top of me with both hands around my throat and I was growing weaker by the second.

I reached over to the nightstand with my left-hand straining for my weapon, but it was too far away. Reaching for something, anything, I grabbed the lamp and slammed it against the right side of his head with all the force I could muster. He fell to the floor beside the bed and blood was running down the side of his face.

He was stunned, but only for a few seconds and quickly recovered twisting himself to his feet.

I was still lying on the bed gasping for air trying to get my wind back. He pulled his gun from his holster, started towards me and I knew I was going to die. I rolled towards the nightstand reaching out for my weapon, but before I could reach it, I heard a gunshot and then a second.

I looked down at my nude body, but I wasn't bleeding. I looked over to where the killer had been standing and he was lying on the floor in a pool of blood. Standing in the doorway of the bedroom was my partner with his gun pointed in the direction of Sean Brooks body. He strolled over and felt Sean Brooks neck for a pulse and said, "He's dead Faye-Lynn."

Dominick holstered his weapon, took off his jacket and approached me. Wrapping the jacket around my nude body he hugged me and asked, "are you ok partner?"

"Yes, thanks to you, he was going to kill me Dominick."

Dominick hugged me and said, "he won't be killing anyone else, it's over."

CHAPTER 56

DETECTIVE THOMAS CALLED Chief Burns to report the shooting, "Chief I need you to get forensics over here right away to Faye-Lynn's house, I just shot Sean Brooks."

"You did what."

"I went to Faye-Lynn's to check on her and as I approached the front door, I heard a loud scream. I rushed inside and followed the sounds upstairs. I walked into Faye-Lynn's bedroom and Sean Brooks was pointing a gun at her. I had no choice, he would have shot her if I hadn't fired first."

"I'm on my way don't do or touch anything until I get there."

"10-4, Chief."

The Chief contacted the forensic investigators from the State Police and asked them to meet him at Detective Johnson's house. He then radioed Squad Lead Patrolman Charlie Reed and explained that there had been an officer involved shooting and he wanted him on the scene as soon as possible.

Chief Burns arrived at the scene and asked Detective Thomas to surrender his badge and weapon until the investigation was over and it was determined that it was a good shooting. "Now, walk me through what happened here Detectives?"

I began to explain, "I came home and discovered Sean Brooks in my bedroom closet, and he tried to kill me. He probably would have if Dominick hadn't showed up when he did. He tried to strangle me at first and I fought him off as best I could, but then he pulled a gun and was going to shoot me."

The forensic investigators had arrived, "Are you ready for us Chief?"

"Sure, come on in. Let's move our conversation downstairs detectives and let the forensic people do their thing," Chief Burns instructed.

We followed the Chief down to the dining room, and I was shaking like a leaf. I still hadn't gotten over the fact that someone had tried to kill me and was lying in the middle of my bedroom floor dead.

"Charlie, I need you to take the detectives statement's and don't leave anything out guys," Chief Burns ordered.

I sat down at the dinning room table and began to describe the horror that I'd just gone through. Patrolman Reed took down every word on a yellow notepad and when we were finish, he said, "I'll need you both to come to HQ tomorrow morning to sign your statements."

"No problem," I replied, and Dominick nodded his head in agreement.

The coroner was called to pick-up Sean Brooks body after the forensics people had completed their work. Most of the other investigators had left when Chief Burns approached me and said, "you should let one of the paramedics check you out Faye-Lynn?"

"I'm fine Chief, really I'm ok."

"What about you Dominick? It's not every day you shoot someone?"

"I'm good Chief," he replied.

"I'm glad it's over, according to his journals, he committed his first murder back in 1978. He killed his mother with a pillow, and no one even suspected that she had been murdered. We'll need to notify the families that we can officially close these cold cases for good."

"I looked over at my partner and smiled. I had just discovered a newfound respect for him, he'd just save my life and suddenly "I got your back" had a whole new meaning to me.

Dominick, you'll need to take administrative leave for a couple of weeks until the investigation over. Faye-Lynn, you should also take some time off. In fact, after these cases I think I'll go on vacation myself."

"Oh yeah, where you are heading Chief," I asked.

"I think I'll take Sandy and the kids to Ocean City Maryland for some much-needed beach time.

The End

Thank you for taking the time to read "The Lipstick Murders," if you enjoyed it, please consider telling your friends or posting a short review on www.amazon.com/author/rickycorumbooks. Word of mouth is an author's best friend and very much appreciated.

Thank you, *Ricky Corum*